P9-DNE-235

THE RECKONING

GEORGES SIMENON

The Reckoning

Translated from the French by
EMILY READ

A Helen and Kurt Wolff Book
Harcourt Brace Jovanovich, Publishers
San Diego   New York   London

Copyright © 1948 by Editions Gallimard
Translation copyright © 1984 by Georges Simenon

All rights reserved. No part of this publication
may be reproduced or transmitted in any form or
by any means, electronic or mechanical, including
photocopy, recording, or any information storage
and retrieval system, without permission in
writing from the publisher.

Requests for permission to make copies of any
part of the work should be mailed to: Permissions,
Harcourt Brace Jovanovich, Publishers, Orlando,
Florida 32887.

LIBRARY OF CONGRESS CATALOGING IN PUBLICATION DATA

Simenon, Georges, 1903–
 The reckoning.

 Translation of: Le bilan Malétras.
 "A Helen and Kurt Wolff book."
 I. Title.
PQ2637.I53B513   1984   843′.912   84-11524
ISBN 0-15-175980-4

Printed in the United States of America

B C D E

1

Emile, the waiter at the Cintra, was struck by the change—and was more or less right in what he made of it. When Malétras came in just after five and sat down behind the bridge players, Emile went up to him as usual, and as usual murmured:

'Good evening, Monsieur Malétras. An Imperial?'

Jules Malétras had not answered—sometimes he did not bother to. Perhaps his mind was on the gentlemen's game of bridge.

In any case, it did not matter. Emile, his thoughts on the customer at table seven, who was showing signs of impatience, dashed over to the high mahogany bar where the barman had already placed a glass on a silver tray, pressed in passing one of the cash register keys, caught the slip of paper and only stopped when he reached the barrel labelled 'Porto Imperial'. The barrel was set in to the wall at the back of the café, where the sunlight's syrupy reflection shone on the woodwork. A rich ruby liquid flowed from the tap.

At that very moment the small pantry door opened and the maid entered and carried a large tray of anchovy canapés over to the bar. Emile looked at the tempting morsels on a bed of hard-boiled eggs, then at Malétras, who was paying no attention to him. For no particular reason, he snatched a small saucer of the canapés and put them on the tray next to the glass.

'Here you are, Monsieur Malétras.'

Malétras, his thoughts obviously elsewhere, looked blankly at the anchovies. Then he raised his eyes towards Emile, who, like all waiters, had by force of habit become no more than a familiar object. It was as though he had suddenly realised that Emile, with his pink sugar complexion, pitted by chicken pox, and his pale-blue eyes, was a human being. Malétras gave him an almost questioning look, as, because of the odd presence of the anchovies on the rectangular tray, something clicked in his mind. 'He's a human being and he wants to please me because I too am a human being.'

Did this really happen, in a fleeting moment in that ray of

1

sunlight? Certainly something took place that Emile had never seen before. Malétras's features appeared to soften; the lower half of his face relaxed in a faint attempt at a smile.

This tentative smile, which partially succeeded, was not a figment of Emile's imagination—Emile was, after all, simply a waiter—because just then Doctor Verel, sitting opposite Malétras, looked up from his cards and was so surprised by what he saw that he mentioned it to the others after Malétras had left.

Emile, on his way to the customer at table seven, who was clearly waiting for a woman and was losing patience, picked up a newspaper, meaning to give it to him, while thinking: 'Monsieur Malétras must be in trouble. I've thought so for some time.'

It seemed inconceivable that the trouble could be of a sexual nature. Nor financial, since everybody in Le Havre knew that Malétras was rich and had retired from business. What catastrophe could befall a rich man of sixty? The worst, surely, must be the worried face of a doctor who, as you are getting dressed, says: 'Yes, well, my friend . . . your heart's getting weak . . . You'll have to . . .'

Or the liver. Or the kidneys. When people are ill, they look at others in a different way—they try to guess their problems, they sympathise with them. Sometimes when men know they are doomed they become very gentle with everybody, and even with animals and objects.

This, more or less, was what Emile thought, without attaching any great importance to it. Curiously enough, Malétras too wondered for a few moments, as he watched the waiter's white jacket go by: 'What can his private life be? Does he have a wife, children, a mistress? Does he have a vice?'

It was the beginning of May, a Saturday. But even on Saturdays the Cintra had none of the bustle of the large cafés. It remained a discreet oasis in the middle of town, with the somewhat sombre decor that Malétras liked—dark panelling, copper, pewter. The awning above the three or four barrels that served as tables out in front was dark red. At five o'clock the sun was no longer hot. It was just warm enough for the customers to appreciate a cool breeze.

Malétras saw all this and himself too as clearly as in a mirror. At that moment, he rather perceived himself as the central figure in *The Drapers' Guild*, a reproduction of which had hung in his dining room for the past forty years.

2

There they sat in a corner of the Cintra, their corner, the corner that was always reserved for them, five men of substance and maturity who had struggled—some more painfully than others—up the ladder of life and had now reached the top.

Who was the man of about thirty, sitting there trembling with impatience, looking at his watch, even though there was a clock right in front of him? It did not matter. Malétras did not know him, but he was certain that, unless the man was a stranger in Le Havre, he must have glanced respectfully towards their table, recognising, no doubt, thin Doctor Verel, the neurologist, possibly also Legrand-Beaujon, of marine insurance, Devismes, of Northern Forests, whose name on advertisements ringed mile after mile of timber yards. He could not fail to recognise the huge, fat, gleaming Steuvels, whose beer was drunk in all the cafés in France, and Malétras himself, of the Malétras Docks, whose olive-green warehouses ruin every village in Normandy.

Forty years earlier Malétras would have been struck dumb before such a group.

Now all he did was pull out his cigar case quite automatically, as he did every day at the same time. It was a grand case of blue morocco edged in gold, with compartments, one for each cigar. Pushing his stomach forward a little, Malétras fumbled at his waistcoat, which had a chain across it, and pulled out of the right-hand pocket a cigar cutter, in the shape of a guillotine, attached to one end of the chain. Finally, he pulled out of another pocket an expensive lighter, gold too, because he liked all these items of everyday use to be made of gold.

He slowly took a few puffs, catching the knowing looks that passed between the card players. He knew what they meant. The same scene had taken place for years. He never offered anyone a cigar. It was not so much from meanness—he did occasionally produce one at home from the pile of boxes on the mantelpiece—as from the fact that his cigar case held his exact supply for the day.

His equipment back in his pockets, he ritually heaved a deep sigh and leaned back a little, half closing his eyes to watch the smoke rise.

He had done all this with the same minute care as ever, but he had done it like a Christian who has lost his faith but still takes the sacraments. He closed his eyes for a second. Luckily, nobody looked at him at that moment: his face expressed infinite sorrow—sorrow for himself, for the wretched Malétras,

3

But then, almost immediately, like someone getting back to business after paying lip service to the emotions, he began to eye Steuvels.

'As soon as he's dummy, I'll catch his eye,' he thought.

He had chosen Steuvels. The doctor was too sarcastic. Legrand-Beaujon, with his squared-off white beard, was too much of an old man. Devismes had eight children.

Steuvels, with his greasy skin and watery eyes, his coarse brutality and often jarring familiarity, whose ruddy flesh spilled out everywhere, was on his third or fourth wife—and rumour had it that he had found this last one in a brothel.

'Three diamonds,' said the doctor. His head shook, from a nervous tic, in quick jerky movements.

'No bid.'

'No bid.'

If Devismes did not say 'Three spades,' and the doctor continued, Steuvels would be dummy, and Malétras would be able to speak to him.

To have stooped to this! His position was worse than that of the poor man over there who had been waiting now for an hour, and who could stand it no longer and was making for the telephone.

What could she be like, this woman who was standing him up? Ugly? Stupid? Perhaps both nasty and stupid? Malétras had no illusions on the subject. He did not despise the lover. He almost hoped to see him emerge from the telephone booth reassured. But when he did reappear, he seemed more agitated than ever and called Emile to bring him some notepaper. He must be married. Perhaps he had children.

'No-trump.'

'Two.'

'Three.'

At last! Steuvels was free, and Malétras got up quickly and put his hand on his shoulder.

'Could you come over here for a moment?'

Why did this remind him of school? All his memories of school, or almost all, were unpleasant. He blushed, as the pale and suspicious child he had been used to blush.

Guiding Steuvels to the back of the café, near the swinging doors leading to the washroom, he found himself facing the terrace which, with its red awning, varnished, copper-banded barrel tables, and the dark-green of the boxed plants around the edges, must have seemed a most attractive refuge to the passers-by.

'Listen, Steuvels . . .'

He must be ashen-faced by now. And yet he tried to reproduce the smile he had raised towards Emile.

'I'd like to ask a small favour. . . . Could you ring my house and tell my wife that we are having dinner together?'

He would much rather have said: 'Look, Steuvels, I'm in a jam. I need to borrow a million . . . right away.'

To have done this properly, his voice and the expression on his face should have been less solemn. He knew that one should ask such favours lightly, with a wink and a tap on the belly.

He had hoped for a wink from Steuvels, who had all the vices and appeared in all the most squalid places; he should have understood.

But the fat fool repeated blankly: 'You want to have dinner with me?'

'No . . . I want this evening to myself. I'll say I'm with you, but if I ring myself. . .'

'What excuse shall I give for not asking Madame Malétras to join us?'

'It's a business dinner. . . . You met a Belgian friend, say. . . .'

'Yes . . . All right.'

Was he looking annoyed and hesitant on purpose? Malétras thought not; he was simply balking at possible complications, worrying about his own cosy peace and quiet. If anyone other than Malétras had asked him to do this it would not have mattered. But Malétras!

'All right . . . What's your number? Come with me. You know, for me, such chores . . . Look, you get the number and then hand me the receiver.'

He had to go through it all and then, the deed done, return with a bad-tempered Steuvels to the waiting players.

'Emile!'

'Yes, Monsieur Malétras. Twelve francs.'

Malétras left, sighing.

'See you tomorrow, gentlemen.'

He did not usually leave at this time, but he could no longer remain still; the calm atmosphere was getting on his nerves. He had half an hour to kill, and nothing to do.

He mingled with the crowds on Rue de Paris, then realised that he was running a constant risk of bumping into Lulu on her

5

shopping spree. She would be quite capable of making him go with her. A tram came by, and he got on, staying on the platform even though he was pushed farther and farther into a corner as more and more people got on.

It might have been midsummer already. The women wore light-coloured hats and dresses. The sidewalk cafés were crowded; one could smell the apéritifs in the air.

The tram headed for the suburbs, where people sat out on their doorsteps. Wherever he went, the sunlight hurt Malétras's eyes. Some streets were flooded with sunlight, others were plunged in shadow and the sunlight appeared mockingly only on a third-floor or attic window. People's skin was warm and damp with the sun of summer. Someone near Malétras smelled of garlic.

How, now, could he recreate the extraordinary life of that winter? It would never be the same again; he knew that. Yet he hung on to hope like the customer at table seven in the Cintra, who was probably still waiting. He lived in turmoil. And the worst of it was that there was never a moment when he was not aware of it.

He had no illusions. He could well imagine Lulu, that afternoon, going from shop to shop with her bag full of money, opening it wide to show the shopkeepers the bundles of notes.

What on earth was she going to buy? She had terrible taste. She was vulgar. She liked only the most common and garish things.

She was aggressive too, and mean. What else might she think up that evening to humiliate him? He had already had to do something he would never have believed possible—humble himself in front of Steuvels!

The tram had arrived at the terminal, and Malétras had to get off. He walked down a long empty street lined with factories and, when the tram caught up with him, he got on again to go back into town. He nearly got off at Place de l'Hôtel-de-Ville, but stayed on as far as the port.

The sun had changed and ruined everything. Nothing was mysterious any more, or even sordid. It was just commonplace. And stupid. Just the teeming background to a grubby life.

During those evenings in winter, he would slip alongside these same walls with the collar of his coat turned up, in an agony of excitement, avoiding the darker shadows, corners from which danger might spring. He knew every gas lamp and the faintly luminous rectangles of small dockside bars. He would turn right, then right again. His heart pounding, he would reach Impasse de la Pie and, right at the bottom, at the end of the cul-de-sac, his feet splashing in puddles, he would go down a damp alley and cross a roughly paved courtyard.

The smell of poverty there caught in the throat. On the ground floor of the building at the end of the yard was a carpenter's workshop. When Malétras got there before six, he would see the carpenter in the greyish light of the bulb that hung from the ceiling. He would climb an outside staircase, bump into a glass door, and be there: Lulu would open the door.

It was not the Lulu of today either. More often than not she would be in a dressing gown, half-naked, always a mess, with her hair all over her face. She always seemed to have just got up from the sofa by the little iron stove, where she spent whole days reading novels with gaudy covers.

'What's in that parcel?'

He would bring her cakes or sweets or chocolates. Never much.

Sometimes Lulu would sulk. She wanted this or that but never anything expensive.

At that time she thought he was a bank clerk.

On other days, she would deliberately pretend to have regrets, and he, the fool, would question her:

'Are you sorry?'

'Of course not.'

'Admit that you miss it a little?'

'Miss what?'

'The café.'

'If you think it's fun being everyone's servant!'

'You used to see a lot of people.'

She was not beautiful. Her features were irregular and she had a pale complexion that moved Malétras, as did her body, which was that of an unhealthy child.

He had met her at the beginning of autumn, in the Café de l'Escale. He had gone in by chance for a drink and she had been working there. She had been wearing a shiny little black serge dress and a white apron. Even now he would sometimes beg her to put it on just for him, in the intimacy of the bedroom.

'Men used to flirt with you. . . .'

'As if I cared about them!'

'Wasn't there one you liked listening to?'

'Men are all the same.'

'What about me?'

7

'You're different.'

He was jealous of her past and would question her for hours, and she would obediently play the game, letting him believe anything he liked, yet never completely reassuring him.

'Did you ever have any lovers?'

'Never.'

'Even when you were very young?'

A memory made her smile.

'At school . . .' she murmured.

'Go on.'

'There was a boy. The Gouel boy. He had red hair. He always wanted to . . .'

'What?'

'Touch.'

'What about you?'

One day, he found a man at her place, tall and thin, with his arm in a sling.

'This is my brother, Joseph. He's a waiter on the *Normandie*. He's on leave now because he's got a sore hand.'

Joseph, who had a permanently spotty face and boils on his neck, was slightly gloomy, pale and shifty.

She and Joseph insisted on teaching him three-handed *belote*. Some evenings, they would take him to play in local bistros where he was not afraid of being recognised.

It was exactly a week ago to the day. . . . He had gone to her room as usual . . . and had found Lulu standing fully clothed, her face drawn and her lips quivering so much that she could not speak for a full minute. 'You . . . you . . .'

He did not understand, and looked around for Joseph, whom he had become used to seeing there.

'Aren't you ashamed?'

And then: 'Aren't you ashamed, Monsieur Malétras?'

The shock was hardly perceptible. He did not even move. And yet he saw that it was all over. Emile, the waiter at the Cintra, had not been far wrong when he was reminded of a man who had just been gently told by his doctor that he was doomed.

'Well?'

'When I think that you, with more money than you can spend, made me live on a thousand francs a month! Look at these dresses you gave me! That's what I've done with them!'

He could not bear to think of it. It was horrible. She had torn

8

up and smashed everything, and he . . . he had cried. He had begged forgiveness. He had knelt in front of her.

Joseph had come back. Had it all been prearranged? Had she deliberately put on her black waitress's dress that evening?

It was Joseph who had intervened on Malétras's behalf.

'Come on, Lulu. He's sorry for what he did. He wasn't thinking. Now he'll make it up to you. . . .'

'I don't need the money. It's not the money I mind; it's the lies.'

And now Malétras was standing in an unknown street looking for the bistro where Lulu had told him to meet her.

One week! He had given her everything he had in his pocket. She had wanted a fur coat. It was not the right season, and he had told her so, but she had always wanted a fur coat.

She had seen one that cost eleven thousand francs.

'Your wife's got a two-hundred-thousand-franc mink, hasn't she?'

But the wealthy Malétras, although he could sign cheques for one or two million francs, could not spend ten or twelve thousand and hide it from Hermine, his second wife, the widow of the general, whom he had married six years earlier.

Even then he had thought of Steuvels. He had thought of all his friends, those at the Cintra and others. And right after that he had bumped into his son-in-law.

What had Lulu said? Picratt's? It was this bright-red place with the twang of a banjo coming through the open door.

Perhaps he was about to play the role of the man he had seen earlier? What did it matter now? He went in. There was a raised bar to the right of the entrance.

'Jules!'

There she was, on a stool, with a cigarette in her mouth. Apart from the barman and the banjo player, she was the only one there, and she had probably been confiding in the barman when Malétras came in.

'Sit down. What do you think?'

She was wearing the famous fur coat, of course, as well as new shoes and stockings. She had been to the hairdresser, and her perm made her look like a doll, a doll he barely recognised.

'Don't you like it?'

'Of course I do.'

'Give him a Manhattan too, Bob. You can see what else I bought later. . . .'

Then in a low voice: 'I spent it all. Are you cross?'

9

'No.'

'You look angry. What's the matter?'

She seemed to be an old friend of the banjo player, and when they were having dinner in a little restaurant with an orchestra, Malétras could not keep himself from making a jealous scene.

He knew that he was off to a bad start. She said, clumsily:

'Are you cross because I spent your twenty thousand francs?'

They argued again because she wanted to spend an hour in a nightclub before going home. He gave in.

At the door of the Cloche, under the mauve neon sign, she went into raptures over a long sports car with shiny bodywork.

'Are we going in or not?' he said impatiently.

What if he bumped into Steuvels, who came to just this kind of place? It was crowded, and the heat made it stifling. Unreal faces in the reddish light, couples squeezed against one another, tables too small and seats too deep.

As he had expected, people asked Lulu to dance. She looked at him questioningly; he remained sullen—but she danced anyway.

And then the catastrophe occurred. There was a tall, athletic man in a grey suit standing at the bar so that Malétras could see only his back. He turned round, and they recognised one another. It was his son-in-law, Etienne Laniel. Laniel thought that his father-in-law was alone and came over.

'You here?' He was surprised.

He was handsome: he had slightly dingy fair hair and a weak face, but he was handsome all the same. Women liked him.

'May I?'

He sat down. Lulu came back.

'Aren't you going to introduce me?'

'My son-in-law. A friend, Lulu.'

Of course. Laniel now understood why his father-in-law had borrowed twenty thousand francs from him.

'What are you doing in Le Havre?' Malétras asked Etienne.

'After dinner I thought I'd try out my new car. . . .'

'Is that it outside?' Lulu exclaimed. 'It must be thrilling to drive in.'

'Would you like a ride?'

'Are you offering?'

'If my father-in-law doesn't mind, I'll take you off for a quarter of an hour.'

Lulu was very animated—she had had two cocktails and a lot of wine at dinner. She quickly downed two glasses of champagne

10

and followed Laniel. When she got to the door, she blew a kiss at Malétras from her fingertips.

A quarter of an hour went by. Malétras was hot. He was suffocating. Every now and then he sighed to himself: 'It's impossible' or 'It's all over.'

The powerful scent of a woman near him made him feel giddy. A hostess came and sat next to him.

He finally went out and waited on the pavement near the doorman, who several times tried to strike up a conversation. He no longer dared look at his watch. They had already been gone more than an hour. More time went by. Every taxi that passed in the distance . . .

At last, the sports car. Lulu jumped out, and had a shock when she saw Malétras there in front of her.

'What's the matter?'

She went into the attack.

'Couldn't you have waited inside? I'm dying of thirst!'

'No.'

'What do you mean, no?'

'Come on.'

He murmured: 'Goodnight, Etienne.'

He no longer knew what he was doing. He dragged her along, holding her arm. She was a little frightened.

'Where did you go?'

'Along the Dieppe road.'

'Did you stop anywhere?'

'Let go. You're hurting me.'

'Tell me where you stopped.'

'Nowhere. We were going a hundred and eighty.'

'And then?'

'And then nothing. Anyway, you bore me. . . .'

'I what?'

'I said you bore me. I've had enough, so there! First you treat me like goodness knows what—leaving me in misery despite all your millions. Then your lordship . . .'

They reached the corner of Impasse de la Pie, and Lulu hesitated.

'I'm not going in,' she suddenly said.

'Go in.'

'What for?'

'Go in.'

11

She nearly refused, but he was stronger and blocked her way out.

'Well, we're not doing anything tonight,' she threw out.

'Why?'

'Because!'

'Why?'

'Oh, hell!'

He followed her in total darkness down the alley. They crossed the yard, and Lulu hesitated once again.

'What's the matter with you tonight?'

'Go up.'

And then, when they were in the room:

'Here I am. Now what do you want from me?'

'You made love with my son-in-law.'

'Fool.'

'Admit it.'

He was completely enraged and suffering the torments of the damned. She was angry too.

'Well, he's much better-looking than you, and at least he's got a car. And he must be rich too, because you borrowed that money you gave me from him.'

'He told you that?'

'I suppose it's not true?'

He could imagine them both laughing at him, with the wind blowing past them on the road.

'Now go back to your wife and leave me alone.'

'Get undressed.'

'No . . . not today.'

He kept coming back to the same question:

'Why not?'

Because she had made love with Etienne, of course.

'Get undressed.'

'No. You're beginning to get on my nerves.'

'Do as I say, or else . . .'

It had become an obsession. He thought that by forcing her to undress he could prove her infidelity. It was nonsense, but this nonsense ruled him in the moments that followed.

'Get undressed.'

'You're hurting me, you imbecile. . . . Can't you see what you look like? Look in the mirror. You look like a lunatic. . . .'

How many times did he say 'Get undressed'?

'You're mad, do you hear? If you keep on like this, I'm going to shout for help. . . .'

He strangled her. When he let go, she fell heavily to the floor and did not move again. Nor did he. Perhaps he felt some sort of relief. He repeated, as he had done in that stifling nightclub earlier: 'It's all over.'

He needed to sit down, and had to move some parcels off a chair—the notorious purchases of that afternoon. He almost drew his cigar case out of his pocket without thinking, because he had a vague feeling that something was missing. Then he heard a noise in the next room, which served as both kitchen and storeroom. The door opened, without startling him.

It was Joseph. So Malétras had been right. He had always thought that Joseph was Lulu's lover, not her brother. He had even resigned himself to it because he felt it was inevitable.

Malétras never knew why he then said, in a curiously calm voice:

'We must call the police.'

The other man turned Lulu's body over and murmured:

'Idiot!'

As thin and pale as a street urchin, Joseph slithered across the floor in his espadrilles to make sure that the curtains were drawn, opened the door, listened, and then came back to the middle of the room.

'Go home, and don't do anything. I'll see to everything.'

Malétras did not understand at once.

'The sooner you get home, the better. Just try to keep your nerve. If you can hang on, there'll be no trouble. Now get out of here.'

He handed him his hat and shut the door behind him. And in the dark alley that linked the courtyard to the street Malétras stopped like a sleepwalker to pee against the wall.

2

Before so much as opening his eyes, Malétras knew that something extraordinary had happened: sunlight, already warm, already thickly golden, was filtering between the slats of the Venetian blinds; he stretched out his hand and felt that the space next to him in bed was cold and empty; the street sounds had organised themselves and replaced the bird song that normally greeted him when he woke up. Ever since he was a small child, since the time when he still had a mother who dressed him and sent him off to the village school, Jules Malétras had always risen at five o'clock in the morning.

On other days he would slip noiselessly from between the sheets, leaving Hermine asleep. Without getting his slippers from the bedside rug, he would go in his nightshirt to the right-hand bathroom; although they had decided to share a bedroom, they had separate bathrooms. Malétras would throw the window wide open. There was nothing opposite. Rue de la Commanderie, where he had chosen to place his new house, in the most elegant part of town, had not been completely developed. There were still gaps between the big private houses, gardens or patches of wasteland. The trees planted along the pavements were young and had light, soft-green leaves.

He had to shut the door carefully, because he had never got into the habit of washing without blowing like a seal. He went downstairs at practically the same time as Eugénie, Hermine's old housekeeper, who said one day:

'I've had no luck with Madame's husbands. The first one, because he was a soldier, was around my feet by six in the morning, with the orderly already holding the horse by the bridle outside the door. Madame marries another gentleman, who's not a soldier, and it has to be one who gets up like country people and eats at the kitchen table.'

What a strange impression everything made on him this morning! He looked at the surroundings he had known for six years and it was exactly as if he was in the most unfamiliar of hotel rooms.

This huge bed, for example, where he lingered for no reason, when he normally never remained between those hateful damp sheets! It was a Louis XVI bed, painted grey, with carved garlands and delicate wickerwork panels, and, to crown it all, a little canopy of satin drapes, hanging from a crown supported by cupids.

It was Hermine's bed. It was not the general's, because in the general's day they slept apart. No doubt it was a matter of social class. Hermine's maiden name was Hermine de Dodeville.

Malétras had never slept apart from his first wife, Louise, who was a Belloncle. They had had only one bathroom for the two of them. In the beginning, they had not had a bathroom at all, or a

14

lavatory, or running water. They had washed themselves in an enamel basin on a three-legged wooden stand.

Why did he and Hermine not sleep separately, as had been the case with the general? They said 'vous' to each other. They had never said 'tu.' Throughout the day they lived together like people who hardly knew one another. And that was true in a way, since, when they married, Hermine was fifty-three and he was fifty-five.

They had never thought about what their sleeping arrangements would be. They had decided that the marriage would take place as soon as the house on Rue de la Commanderie was built.

'Tomorrow, Hermine, if you will permit me, I will send the architect in, because there are some details I would like you to settle with him.'

It was the question of the rooms. She had decided: one bedroom. Two bathrooms, but only one bedroom. Her own bathroom was in pink marble.

Perhaps he was only now discovering the truth: he had woken up, felt the bed next to him, and been seized by physical anguish on finding that he was alone. He felt he could hardly breathe, that his heart was beating irregularly; he was afraid of being ill, of dying without the time or the chance to reach for the bell.

They were both old. At night their loneliness frightened them. During the day, comforted, they could say 'vous' to one another and exchange civilities. At night each needed to feel that the other was sleeping within a hand's reach.

Sitting in bed, he looked at himself in the mirror of the large grey closet opposite, and something on his face triggered a memory: the vague smile he saw, both timid and almost friendly, softening his mouth, slightly blurring his eyes, was the same smile he had turned towards somebody the day before, a man he hardly knew, Emile, the waiter at the Cintra.

He had been feeling wretched even then. It had never occurred to anybody to feel the slightest pity for the powerful Malétras. Nobody gives charity to the rich. Then a stranger, or almost, this waiter to whom he had never paid the slightest attention, had put a saucer of anchovy canapés in front of him, as if to say:

'It may not be much but it gives me pleasure.'

Had Emile suspected that his customer was unhappy? Was Emile unhappy too? Perhaps he was ill? Perhaps he had romantic problems?

Malétras looked for his watch, but it was not on the bedside table where he usually put it. Then he remembered. He had undressed in the dark. He had been afraid of waking up Hermine, afraid particularly of the questions she might ask, looks she might give.

But she had not opened her eyes. He had dropped his clothes on the rug and climbed in next to her. She had automatically drawn away, and automatically mumbled in her sleep:

'Is it late?'

He had answered: 'Midnight.' He did not know if it was midnight; he just said it.

He had foreseen a sleepless night, but had fallen into a deep sleep. He remembered that during the night Hermine had forced him to turn over because he kept sliding against her, and she had said:

'You smell of drink.'

His clothes were no longer on the rug, but neatly on a chair. According to his watch, it was nine o'clock. He wondered why Hermine, who got up late, was no longer in her bathroom. Suddenly worried, he went into his bathroom, put on a dressing-gown, and rang the bell.

Three minutes later—he kept looking at his watch—nobody had yet answered his call. He rang again, for a long time before he heard hurried footsteps on the stairs, coming from the second floor, and finally a ruffled Rose, the little housemaid, appeared.

'Did monsieur ring?'

'Where were you, Rose?'

'Upstairs in the linen room, with madame.'

'What's going on?'

'Nothing's going on, monsieur. Madame decided yesterday to put the second floor in order, and we're starting with the linen.'

'Bring me a cup of coffee.'

He never had it before going downstairs, but he needed to give some reason for having rung the bell.

He had been worried at the prospect of his first meeting with Hermine, of the questions she might put to him, of her more or less perceptive looks, and now he was thrown because she was not there.

How stupid he was, again, to say to Rose when she brought him his coffee:

'Anything new?'

'No, monsieur.'

He felt even more ill at ease once he was dressed. Should he

16

go up to say good morning to his wife? Any other day he would not have done so. They lived their own lives.

He went up just the same, aware of his awkwardness. He found Hermine, with a kerchief around her hair, busy arranging piles of linen.

'You're up?' she said with faintly sarcastic good humour. 'Head not hurting too much?'

'We were with friends.'

'I know, I know. You must have looked charming on your way back. I shall congratulate Steuvels when I next see him. Well? Why are you standing there?'

There was obviously nothing to be done. It was probably the first time he had set foot in the linen room. The sun flooded in, and Hermine, with her neat appearance and precise movements, her fresh complexion and even temper seemed very light and alert, like a nurse in a hospital.

Was it not extraordinary that she was his wife?

'Aren't you going to your office?'

'Yes . . . I'm going. . . .'

'If you see a nice lobster, remember to bring it back.'

This was so different from what he had foreseen! He had not thought about Lulu once since waking up. There was, in a corner of his mind, something dark and slimy, but he avoided it.

His mind was clear. It was probably clearer than usual; he was seeing everything around him with new eyes.

How could he define his uneasiness? He felt unsteady. More precisely, he felt he was outside reality.

That was it! Before, he had been Jules Malétras, the son of the Malétras they called Julot, the postman at Steenvorde. Today, he was Malétras of the Malétras Docks, which he had sold a few years earlier, after the death of his first wife and his daughter's marriage, when he had been seized by a feeling of disgust for business.

In addition, he was the Malétras of Rue de la Commanderie and the Cintra, the Malétras who had made a new life by marrying Hermine and who, to amuse himself, spent two hours every morning at the fish market.

All of that now seemed unreal. He put on his hat, lit his first cigar, left the house, and walked along the pavement, and everything was as blurred as it is on those days spent in the anonymous ambience of a clinic after an operation.

17

He bought a newspaper at the street corner and scanned all the pages, but found nothing about Lulu.

Was he wrong to have left the house? Suppose Joseph rang.

Pictures came into his mind, as they do on the morning after a drinking spree. He pushed them aside, deferring until later the trouble of thinking about them.

Yet even the trams, the bustle of the street, the play of sun and shade—nothing could hold his attention, not even the sight of his old firm at the bottom of Rue de Paris and his name in large red letters: MALÉTRAS DOCKS.

He walked as far as the port. He was only two hundred metres from Impasse de la Pie, but, despite a craving to wander in that direction, he did not dare go there.

His son-in-law! He had forgotten about him. His son-in-law knew that he had gone home with Lulu, and that he had been angry with her.

Malétras walked with his hands in his pockets, as on other days. Coming round a corner, a boy running with a basket bumped into him.

It was in front of a hairdresser's shop. Part of the shop's front was made of mirrors. Malétras caught a glimpse of himself in one of them just as the boy bumped into him. He literally caught himself smiling that same smile, the one directed at Emile the day before and the one that morning in bed, as he mumbled:

'Sorry . . .'

He, Malétras, was apologising to a street boy who had jostled him!

He was furious with himself as he crossed the fish market, and he made himself walk more stiffly and heavily than usual, barely answering with a grunt the greetings of the fishwives and workmen.

In a narrow street behind the markets, which was always jammed with lorries and handcarts, he went into a small glass-fronted office, whose sign read:

POINEAU AND BROTHERS
WHOLESALE FISHMONGERS

He had resumed his icy boss's expression and chewed on his dead cigar. His bowler hat added to the severity of his appearance by seeming to sink down on his forehead.

'Well, Poineau?'

'Yes, Monsieur Malétras.'

Poineau was a big, vigorous young man with blue eyes, who worked as though driven. People always said he never had any luck. The fact was, he couldn't count.

He took money in by the handful, stuffed it in the pockets of his blue overalls, or into drawers, forgot to invoice things, and had reached the point where he was inches away from bankruptcy.

'Come to the office.'

'Yes, Monsieur Malétras.'

He trembled before Malétras, who had saved him by financing him, but who, since then, came every morning and spent two hours in the back of the shop, where a miserable desk had been installed.

'How many boxes this morning?'

'Thirty-two boxes of soles, twenty of . . .'

Malétras was so wealthy that he did not know what to do with his money. He had, out of weariness, sold his business, where in the past he had employed up to thirty people in the office alone, not counting the warehousemen, lorry drivers, stokers, and so on.

Now, for the past three years, each morning, punctually, like one of his own old accountants, he had come to this room, three metres by two, lit only by means of a window above the door. Here, amid the powerful smell of fish, he could spend two hours drawing up bills and entering figures.

He did it that morning as on others, going into the shop ten times to check weighing chits and marks on the boxes. It was nearly twelve when a boy came in with a letter and said:

'Is there a Monsieur Malétras here?'

'That's me. Give me that.'

He was right. He had been expecting to hear from Joseph all morning.

He had never seen his writing before and he was surprised to find it clear and elegant, possibly somewhat too painstaking, like that of a teacher or a sergeant.

I shall need to see you this afternoon without fail. Can you be at the Bar des Amis at four o'clock? It is a small bar on Quai Frissard, near the coal depots. Everything will be all right.

Yours,
Joseph

'Aren't you going to have your rest?' Hermine asked him when she saw him light a cigar while they were still at the table.

19

'I've got to go to the bank. In fact, I wanted to talk to you about it. . . .'

Before him on the wall was the colour reproduction of *The Drapers' Guild*, which he had been thinking of the day before at the Cintra. Rose had just served the coffee in little gold cups. Hermine, as she always did, put a sugar lump in her husband's cup and handed it to him.

'Poineau spoke to me this morning about a colleague of his in Dieppe who deals mainly in lobster . . .'

'I bet you forgot mine.'

He had forgotten, but did not dare admit it.

'They're going to bring it later. I thought it was for this evening. . . . I was saying . . . this colleague is a bit pushed at the moment. . . . The business isn't doing badly—on the contrary—but it's short of capital. . . . By advancing him a hundred thousand francs . . .'

She was listening carefully. Was it not he who at the beginning had insisted on her knowing about his business? It was true also that she came from a family where the women always took an early interest in their investment.

'Do you think it's worth saddling yourself with new worries? You'll have to go to Dieppe.'

'No. Poineau will go.'

'You know perfectly well you wouldn't trust him. And I know you; you'd insist on seeing everything for yourself. You hate journeys, and you'd insist on taking me. For my part . . .'

He was forced to invent a whole story, to lie as he had done to his mother when he was a child.

'I promised I'd invest at least a hundred thousand francs in the business. If, in the first few months . . .'

'You shouldn't have promised anything without asking me first.'

He went, as he had said, to the bank, where he drew out a hundred thousand francs in thousand-franc notes. Arriving in the centre of town too early, he tried to sit in a café, but he could not stay still, so he walked at random. He found himself on Quai Frissard by half past three, but avoided going near the yellow-painted bar he saw at the end of a long black wall.

He had thought of enclosing the hundred thousand francs in an envelope and handing it to Joseph, saying:

'There.'

And it would all be over.

It was absurd; things happened quite differently. Joseph too arrived much earlier than he had said. Malétras did not see him come. He suddenly heard a voice next to him saying:

'I didn't make you wait, did I?'

It was Joseph, neatly dressed, with a soft hat, not a cap, on his head. His arm was no longer in a sling, but one finger was still bandaged.

'It might be better if we didn't sit down in a bar. I gave you this address so as not to make you wait on the pavement.'

Malétras said nothing, not daring to look his companion in the face. He fingered the bank notes in his pocket.

'Shall we walk along the quay? I sent you that note this morning mainly to reassure you.'

Malétras finally looked at him. Joseph was pale, but that was his normal colouring. There was no arrogance in his expression or his posture; on the contrary, there was a certain humility, more the sort of deference Malétras might have expected from one of his employees.

He was proper—that was the right word. Proper in his dress and in his speech.

'I wanted to tell you too that I'm leaving Le Havre this evening.'

'I brought . . .'

The other man understood at once and protested:

'Oh! It's not what you think. The thing to avoid—isn't it?—is anyone wondering where she is.'

Although he had not mentioned Lulu's name, Malétras knew what he meant.

'I don't think the landlady will wonder, because I took everything away. With rooms of that kind, people often do a moonlight flit, and we didn't owe her much, so she won't bother to tell the police. We should walk.'

'Sorry . . .'

Again! Was he now going to apologise like this at every turn—he who had never apologised to anyone before?

'The most difficult thing is her parents, because she used to write to them, maybe once a week, and sometimes one of her brothers or sisters would come and see her here. They must be written to immediately. That's why I'm leaving. I've chosen Nice, because it's a long way away. I must go to Paris first to see somebody who is essential to us. . . .'

The 'us' made Malétras wince as he gazed at the boats being unloaded in the sun.

'He's an educated fellow who mostly makes fake identity cards

21

and passports. I don't know him personally, but I've heard about him. Apparently he can imitate handwriting well enough to fool everybody. I've got some examples for him. He'll copy Lulu's writing, and she'll supposedly write to her parents that she's in Nice, and then somewhere else, always further away. You understand?'

He spoke plainly and this simplicity was surprising.

'You see I'm doing what I can. This man charges two thousand for a fake passport. I think that if we offer him a thousand francs per letter, he'll co-operate.'

'I've brought money.'

'Wait. I'll make him write four or five letters in advance. Say five. Five thousand francs. I'll go and post the first ones in Nice. I've found out how much it costs to get there. In third class. . . '

'There's a hundred thousand in this envelope .'

'That's too much. You haven't understood me. I don't want to take your money. Just what's necessary. Let's say five thousand francs for my expenses and five thousand for the letters.'

'Take it. . . .'

'Be careful. People are watching. . . . I tell you, you're offending me. . . . What I've done is for you. . . .'

They were bathed in sunlight, cranes went on working, sacks fell onto the dock in clouds of luminous dust.

'Just give me ten thousand francs. If I need more, I'll write to you or come and see you. Don't worry, I won't write to you at home, but at Poineau's. I'll just sign with a *J*. You'll understand.'

'Are you sure . . .' Malétras began.

The words wouldn't come out. What he wanted to ask was if . . .

'I understand. Don't be afraid. She won't be found. . . .'

Seeing that his companion remained still, almost paralysed, like a sick man waiting for the onset of an approaching attack, Joseph quickly went on:

'What are you thinking? It wasn't your fault! I often told her she was going too far. Believe me, it wasn't out of wickedness. She couldn't help it. She was fooling around. Here! Take the rest. I only need ten notes. I insist. Otherwise you'll imagine things that aren't true.'

Where did they part company? Malétras had no idea. In the bottom of his pocket his right hand still clutched a handful of notes. He walked, crossed bridges, passed docks and quays,

22

without daring to turn round for fear of seeing Joseph's silhouette behind him.

Suddenly he stopped dead. A funeral was going by, a pauper's hearse, with only a man and a child following it. He said clearly:

'Lulu.'

Then he was seized with panic. He realised that if he went on like this he would be lost.

He must at all cost become himself, Malétras, again.

Where was Joseph? No doubt he had rushed to the station and was waiting for his train.

And Lulu . . . The night before, at the same time . . .

'Give me a glass of water, please.'

He had gone into a bar. He started when he saw a sickly little waitress appear from behind the counter, a girl like Lulu, who looked at him, surprised, and asked:

'Is there something wrong?'

As if to put him at his ease, thinking that here was an old man who was ill, she continued:

'It happens to a lot of people with these first hot days, when you're not expecting them. . . .'

He smiled at her. He was ashamed of that smile. He was angry with himself. He looked for change in his pocket but couldn't find any.

'It's all right. I'm not going to charge for a glass of water, really!'

Somebody had given him a glass of water—him! Malétras! And he had said thank you! He had turned round to say thank you! Was he going to become good?

He felt somewhat steadier. He managed not to think about Joseph any more, or to hear his monotonous, oversoft voice. Why had the boy appeared so proper and reserved?

He had prepared a hundred thousand francs, and now he was going to be encumbered with the ninety thousand he had left.

Hermine was busy cleaning and tidying the second floor with the maids. The previous week they had spring-cleaned the first floor. Next week would be the ground floor's turn.

He went back into the centre of town, and because it was the right time he went towards the Cintra. He had to go there anyway. He must not change any of his habits.

There were two lovers holding hands behind the green plants in the tiny space beneath the crimson awning.

The bay windows were wide open, and the four bridge players

were there, in their places, with the pink faces of well-tended old men.

Emile rushed forward to take his hat, and Malétras was on the point of smiling, but he caught himself and gave a grunt instead.

Steuvels, facing him, thought he should give a conspiratorial wink. Malétras shrugged his shoulders and sat down without saying anything, because that was the tradition; he leaned back a little and pulled out of his pocket the cigar case edged in gold, and then, from his waistcoat, the guillotine-shaped cigar cutter.

It never failed: at the moment he pressed the lighter, the others exchanged a glance, the famous daily glance, the joke that never grew stale, that never would, and Malétras, blowing the blue smoke out in front of him, said to himself:

'Fools!'

And that idiot Emile, who, just because he had once been thanked with a smile, rushed up like an overfriendly dog to bring him a saucer of anchovy canapés!

3

It could not be long after half past nine. They had finished eating some time ago and, as they did every night, they had gone into the little room adjoining the large drawing room. The servants called it the boudoir. Malétras, who did not care for the word, avoided mentioning the room or just said: 'Shall we go through?' As for Hermine, she said simply: 'My room.'

This came about because, when Malétras had had the house on Rue de la Commanderie built, with a view to their marriage—the idea of marriage and that of the house were so closely linked that they had never imagined one without the other—one question had arisen, that of the furniture. They each had their own furniture. Malétras's was heavier, solid oak or walnut, rather dark, because he liked the feeling of solidity that old woodwork conveyed.

Hermine, or the general's wife, as some still called her, had very different furnishings. They were a mass of small antique pieces like those now gracing this room, marquetry, bonheurs-du-jour, desks with hidden drawers and folding tops, which hardly seemed able to balance on their slender legs. There was also modern Louis XVI, as in their bedroom. She had brought with her the chandelier in the large drawing room too, but the furniture there was new: they had chosen it together.

She was writing. Malétras was sitting in a tapestry-covered tub chair, the only one in which he was allowed to spread himself out with his waistcoat unbuttoned, as he did every evening. He read his newspapers, or, rather,this evening he pretended to read them, recognising a word or item here and there, turning the pages with the usual sighs. In fact, he was thinking.

What he was thinking, as he lifted his head and looked at his wife over the top of the paper, was:

'What would she do if I told her everything?'

All his friends had said to him over and over again:

'Hermine is a remarkable woman.'

To start with, she had a natural elegance and was at home anywhere. Not only was she at ease herself, but she put everybody else at ease as well.

She was gentle. She never raised her voice. She would just shake her head, and her annoyance was tinged in advance with indulgence.

'Really . . . What are you doing?'

She always dressed in pale, soft colours, and her face was pink beneath her almost-white hair; in the evening when she sat in front of her desk she wore large tortoise-shell-framed glasses. She dealt with the household accounts, tradesmen, properties—she possessed several properties in the country. Or she corresponded with those friends she had remained in touch with. Every evening she would say to Malétras, whom she never ceased to impress:

'Aren't you going to smoke?'

What would she do if, there and then, he quite simply told her about Lulu's death?

She liked looking after others, whether it was he or servants or animals. She liked giving people infusions and medicines. But suppose he said:

'At this minute I should be in prison. Because I have killed, I am no longer officially a part of the human community.'

In a curious way he felt reassured. He was strong enough to think that and not say anything, to continue smoking his cigar and pretending to read. He had got through his first day as a murderer without a hitch, and the first, he imagined, must be the hardest.

One must get used to it as one gets used to anything. So, since he had held on for the first day, the danger must have passed.

The most difficult hours of the day, he now realised, would be those he used to spend with Lulu, when he left the Cintra at about half past five to go to Impasse de la Pie, returning to Rue de la Commanderie only a little before eight o'clock, when dinner was served.

Today he had nearly stayed at the Cintra with the others. But was it not unwise to change his habits in the slightest, allowing people to guess that there was now an empty space in his day?

Actually, when a little after half past five he had found himself alone in the street, he had been on the point of giving up. He did not know where to go. He had to make an effort not to go automatically towards small, narrow streets, to which he had gone throughout the winter at this time of day. He was exhausting himself by this endless walk through the busy streets. He was hot. Sweat broke out on his face. He suddenly felt old. He dared not sit down at the first possible café. He felt it might be dangerous to do so, that he would not know what to say if somebody he knew found him sitting at a table.

The problem was physical, rather than mental. The lack of a corner to shelter in. He nearly got on the tram, as he had done the day before, but it would be even more compromising to be seen in a neighbourhood he had no business to be in.

So at about half past six, really too tired to wander any farther, he went into a bistro in a little street swarming with children. He had never entered this sort of bar before and he was surprised to find clean tables and a zinc counter. There were no customers. One could wonder why there would ever be any. A woman with swollen legs came out of a kitchen where canaries sang, painfully dragging her slippers. She showed no surprise, although she could not have been used to seeing people like him in her place.

'What can I get you?'

He would have liked water, as he had done earlier, in another bistro, but that too would be a mistake.

'It's hot,' he murmured, to give himself time to think, because he did not like alcohol.

'Anisette with water? That's always the best thing in this sort of weather.'

Well! He was almost sure that he would come back here every day and drink an anisette. The woman sat near him, mending a napkin. In the street, one could hear the shouts of the children

26

and the trams ringing their bells to get through the cross-streets, but once inside the door the silence was so complete that the ticking of a cuckoo clock in the kitchen could be heard.

He remained there for three quarters of an hour. He drank two anisettes, so as not to spend too much time in front of one glass. He noticed that the woman was giving herself one behind the counter, and he thought:

'Tomorrow I'll buy her one, to get in her good graces.'

Who knows? She might not be surprised if he said, point-blank: 'I strangled a girl.'

Of course he would not say it. He had no desire to talk about it, but it was comforting to know that it would be possible at any given moment. . . .

'The doorbell,' Hermine said quietly, lifting her head.

They exchanged looks. Malétras was surprised and tried to assume an almost too indifferent expression.

'I wonder if the servants heard.'

They had, because the door opened and then shut; footsteps echoed in the hall with the five marble steps, and Rose came in, closing the door behind her.

'It's monsieur's nephew, who wants to see monsieur.'

'Which nephew?'

'Monsieur Philippe.'

'Why didn't you bring him in?' Hermine interrupted. 'Did you leave him in the hall?'

'I wasn't sure. . . .'

Philippe came in. He was a thin young man, nervous, with small sharp eyes and a tense manner. He was dressed in black and had long hair, like a poet.

'Good evening, Aunt. Good evening, Uncle. I'm sorry to disturb you. . . .'

'Sit down.'

'It's . . . I haven't very much time. . . . I wonder if I could speak to you alone for a minute, Uncle?'

He had probably had to get up his courage before ringing the bell. He seemed uncertain. Had he ever set foot in this house? Malétras wondered. Possibly once, in the early days? But never in the sitting room, which he could not help glancing around at curiously.

'Can't you speak in front of your aunt?'

'Really!' Hermine said. 'He wants to speak to you alone. . . .'

Philippe was not Hermine's nephew. Nor, indeed, was he a Malétras. . . . With him, a whole rather painful past, a world that Malétras hated, entered the house.

Malétras did not like the poor. Not only did he not like them, he had a horror of them. He could have borne the really poor, wretches in rags who form part of the background of little streets in some quarters. He made an exception too for people like his father, the country poor, labourers who live in shanties with their urchins, and work by the day on farms or for the well-to-do.

His hatred was directed at the other poor, amongst them his first wife's family. Philippe was her nephew.

'Come.'

He led him with a heavy, almost threatening step into his office; although he no longer worked, he still had an office, across the hallway.

'Come in. Sit down. What do you want now?'

The 'now' was intentional. The young man had never personally asked for anything, but all the rest of his family—his mother, his aunts, his uncles—had always latched on to Malétras.

They all lived in clean, cramped houses. They dressed correctly. The women would never have gone out without hats and gloves. They put on airs. The children had to go to the best schools; they had to be properly educated. Yet, when all was said and done, they were always chasing after the money they were short of.

The study was dark because Malétras wanted it like that, because ever since he began he had always worked in a dark room. Moreover, the furniture was the same as he had had at the beginning, the green filing cabinets, the desk with its inset rectangle of green imitation leather, and the round-backed chair, which fitted Malétras's back exactly.

'Listen, Uncle. . . . You know I am at the Veron bank. . . . I earn my living. . . . I am a serious person. . . .'

Malétras hated young people. Especially this kind—pale, nervous teenagers who always seem to be in the grip of some fever, who speak with suppressed energy because they believe themselves destined for great things.

'Does your mother know you're here?'

'No. I didn't tell her.'

'And your father?'

Another of those insufferable men, a solemn and priggish accountant who always seemed to be saying:

'But I, sir, am an honest man!'

28

Were these fools now going to become dishonest into the bargain? Anyhow, they would not succeed. People like this . . . Malétras had employed dozens and dozens of them. From time to time one would come into his office, stiff and shaking, both proud and humble:

'Believe me, sir, this is a painful step I'm taking today. It's the first time in my life . . .'

He would gaze coldly at the man, chewing his cigar and with his hat screwed down on his head.

'You know my wife gave birth last month. The baby. . . '

So what? Babies were made to be ill. So were women. All women at some time or other have something wrong with their insides. An operation was necessary? Hospital? Then what? Was it any of his business?

'If you could just lend me a thousand francs, which I would repay at one hundred francs per month . . .'

'Tell me, my friend. . . .'

The man would tremble with hope.

'Do you have too much to live on with what I pay you?'

'No, sir. You know I don't.'

'I don't know anything. I give you so much per month in exchange for the work you do for me. Is it too much, yes or no?'

'No.'

'In that case, how do you expect to live with a hundred francs less per month? It's impossible; you said so yourself. It's not my fault. I'm sorry. You wanted a child, didn't you? What's more, it's the second time in a fortnight that you've asked if you could leave early. . . .'

Philippe, who stood before him twiddling his felt hat, was about to ask for money, he could tell.

'Have you done something stupid?'

'No, Uncle. It's not at all what you're thinking. I hesitated for a long time before coming, but it's a matter of life or death. . . . I must have five hundred francs this evening.'

'And you thought I'd give it to you?'

'I'll pay you back in two months, perhaps sooner.'

'Listen, Philippe. You'll probably say, like all the rest, that I'm a miser. But it's not avarice. It's a principle. I have never lent money in my life. Your mother and aunts know that well. When I had my business, I said to them:

' "Come to the shop as often as you like. You can have as

much as you like at the wholesale price. It'll save you quite a lot each month. But no more credit for you than for anyone else." '

'It's not the same thing,' Philippe mumbled.

'What's not the same?'

'I don't need the money for myself.'

'Who's it for?'

'I just said that it was a matter of life or death.'

'All young people say that. You'll see; she won't kill herself.'

'Who?'

'Your girlfriend, I assume. One of your cousins has already been to tell me all that.'

'What did he tell you?'

'Your story, the story of all boys your age. Your girlfriend is pregnant, isn't she? She's an honest girl. Her parents aren't rich. Maybe her mother does sell herrings in the street, but they're honest people. And you were the first. You're sure you were the first. So if you can't find the money to get rid of it . . .'

'It's not that! I swear it's not that!'

Earlier, when he heard the doorbell, Malétras had been afraid. Did he not have everything to fear from an unexpected visit?

Now he was not only reassured, but also actually pleased with himself. With good reason. The night before, at the same time . . .

Well, less than twenty-four hours later, here he was in his comfortable old chair, in full possession of his faculties. Facing this nephew, who was no longer his nephew, since his first wife was dead, he was exactly the same Malétras whom everybody had always known, before whom so many had trembled.

He wished Emile, the waiter at the Cintra, could see him. Because God knows what Emile had thought when he saw him smiling like a timid and respectable woman. How could he have smiled like that? It had happened three times. He had smiled to himself like that, twice, as if to sympathise, to take pity on himself.

What pity? Eh? What pity?

'If it's not that, you don't need five hundred francs. Or else you've been dipping into the till at the bank and you . . .'

'Uncle!'

'What do you mean, "Uncle"?'

He had done the same himself in the past. A lot of young people did it or were tempted to. If they didn't, it was only because they were afraid. But afterwards, most got frightened and let themselves be caught.

That was what disgusted Malétras, all those weak unhealthy people who think they are honest just because they are afraid!

'I swear on my mother's head. . . .'

'Leave your mother out of this.'

She was another who always complained and thought that life had been unfair, when in fact she had just the life she deserved. Didn't everybody have the life they deserved?

'I swear that I have done nothing wrong.'

'That's your bad luck.'

'What do you mean?'

'Nothing. I don't mean anything. You're the one who rings my doorbell like a madman and comes asking me for five hundred francs.'

The boy's lips quivered, as if he was about to cry.

'Oh, well. Will you promise to keep it a secret?'

'If you insist on your secret, keep it to yourself.'

'Read this letter.'

'You want me to read it? Notice that I didn't ask.'

He was handed an already crumpled piece of paper, and Malétras pulled out of his pocket the lorgnette he needed to read with.

'It's from the son of one of your friends.'

Malétras did not listen. He read:

My dear Philippe,

You must have wondered what had become of me and why I suddenly disappeared without telling you. You must know that it is not my fault, and that by writing I am not entirely sticking to my promise.

I already told you that my father had found Jeanne's letters, but since he did not say anything about them, I did not know what attitude he would take towards her.

He said nothing for a week. I noticed only that he seemed sad and that he had more attacks during meals.

The day before yesterday he called me into his study right after supper, after telling my sister she could go to bed.

He put the letters on the table.

'I wanted to find out more before speaking to you,' he began in a voice I hardly recognised. 'I swear to you, Jean, that if this person was worthy of you, I would have said, today: "Marry her." It would have saddened me, because you're too young to

31

marry, and it would have seriously jeopardised your career, but I would have done it.'

You know my father. Particularly since Mother's illness, he loves us more than any father has ever loved his children. Even though he tries not to discriminate between my sister and me, I feel that I especially am the one who represents everything for him.

He continued in that weak voice, which was painful to hear:

'You can believe me, Jean, when I say that I would only have thought of your happiness. The girl's background, her family, or her money would not have worried me. I have made serious enquiries, and I can tell you she is not worthy of you. She may have made a young and inexperienced man believe anything she wanted, but she had to confess the truth to me. She had lovers before you; she told me so, crying. She had lived for almost a year off one of them, whose name I can tell you if you insist. . . .'

I couldn't say anything, because I knew it. But you know too that none of that matters to me, that the past is the past and that Jeanne will be my wife, whatever she may have done before she knew me.

I did not dare say that to my father, who then told me what he had decided. Since I had a slight recurrence of my pleurisy last month, he has sent me to the Mont Revard for two months, where I was two years ago.

'You must give me your word,' he said, 'not to try to correspond with her. I trust you. I know that if you promise, you'll keep your promise. I have told Jeanne about your departure. She agreed with me that it was necessary. In any case, I left her with some hope, however slender. In a few months, when you have had time to think, and when she, on her side, is living alone once more, we will reopen the matter.'

What can I say, my dear Philippe? My father is ill. The doctor said to me again two months ago that he must have no excitement. I accepted his condition. I left. That evening! He helped me pack and took me to the station. I think that he was as upset as I was when we parted.

Malétras raised his eyes and gazed at his quivering nephew.
'Well!'
'Read it.'

I understand now that I will never be happy and that my father will never consent. I am alone at the hotel, because the season has not begun. Yesterday I walked all day and I stopped for a long time on a rock that was completely pink. I shall go back there this evening. I shall probably go back tomorrow. From there, you can see the whole of Lac du Bourget, and when I stare at the opal-shaded water, I feel dizzy. I feel . . . I know that one evening I won't be able to resist it and that my feet will give way.

It will be for the best. They will think it was an accident. You alone will know the truth. You will tell Jeanne and . . .

'I know Jean. He will kill himself.'

Malétras looked at him attentively, and the young man once more felt hopeful. He did not know that his uncle was thinking of another letter, that he was looking for another face in his nephew's features.

He too had had a son, a son and a daughter, exactly like the father in the letter. His daughter did not count. She was married to that fool Laniel. Malétras had done everything for her. He had given her a magnificent dowry. He had built her, near Caen, one of the most beautiful villas in the region. For a year, immediately after the sale of his business, he had gone to live with her and his son-in-law. He had become a grandfather. It was at their house that he had met Hermine.

What had happened when he announced his intention of remarrying? His daughter had gone to all kinds of lawyers and made every possible difficulty for him. They no longer saw one another. If he met Laniel, when he came to Le Havre for some fun, it was without her knowledge.

But his son! He was handsome. He looked distinguished. He did not look like Malétras, but like his mother. Everybody loved him. He had everything to look forward to. For him, his father would have amassed all the millions anyone could wish for.

He had died, not at the Mont Revard, but in Switzerland, where doctors had sent him. He had died at nineteen, with none of his family near him, while Malétras, in Le Havre, was working hard for his sake.

It was only two years later, by chance, when he was going through his son's things for the tenth time, that he found a little notebook where the boy had written, next to some poems of his own, some thoughts:

'How sad that we cannot choose our parents as we choose our friends! And must we carry throughout our lives the mark of those who brought us into the world?

'From my mother I will always retain a taste for suffering, because she was so unhappy that tears became a sort of opium for her.

'But have I really got my father's imprint on my flesh and my spirit? I sometimes wonder, with terror. I dread discovering in myself . . .'

Malétras had closed his eyes, and Philippe, shaking, dared not break into this unexpected trance. At last, the eyelids opened and a cold look was turned upon the young man.

'What do you want?'

'He's your friend Gancel's son, Uncle. He's my best friend. He's like a brother to me. I know that if he's left alone there, he'll do what he says. I know too that if I went, if I could talk to him . . .'

'Has he got a little blond moustache?'

'Yes. He's twenty-two. He was studying law, but he couldn't continue because of his health. . . .'

'You're asking me for five hundred francs to go there?'

'Yes. I've asked for five days off from the bank. My suitcase is ready. There's a train just before midnight.'

'I bet you've already left your suitcase at the station.'

'Yes.'

'Did you tell your parents that you were coming to ask me for money?'

'No.'

'Why?'

Philippe said nothing, lowered his head.

'Why? You don't dare answer? Because your parents hate me, that's why. Admit it.'

'Perhaps they don't like you.'

'Because I'm rich and they're poor! Because every single member of your family, without exception, has come crying to me at one time or another, like you're doing now.'

'I'm not crying.'

'You're begging.'

'It's not for me.'

'It's for your fool of a friend who think he's the hero of some romance. As for you, you know why you want to go there? I'll tell you. First, because it amuses you to participate in a dramatic

34

story. You take yourself seriously. You're playing a part. Then, it'll be very nice to spend five days away from the boredom of the office; you'll be thrilled by the journey, the night train, crossing Paris, and finally seeing the mountains, which you've never done before.'

'Give me back my letter.'

'Have you given up? Don't you want the money any more?'

'No.'

'Are you too proud?'

'I've never been treated like a beggar before.'

'Well, contrary to what you're expecting, I'm going to give you the five hundred francs, or, rather, lend it to you.'

'Thank you, Uncle.'

'You see! A moment ago you didn't want it any more and now you're already saying thank you. But you must sign a receipt and pledge to repay me at the rate of a hundred francs a month.'

'Yes, Uncle.'

'Take some paper. Sit down here. Not that pen; it's mine. The red one. Write "I, the undersigned . . ." '

How Malétras hated the young man at that moment; he could feel him trembling as he placed a heavy hand on his shoulder, as if to give him an even stronger sense of being crushed.

He hated him because he was nineteen, because he had no self-doubt, because he was the nephew of Louise, who had died cursing her husband, and the cousin of Henri, his son, dead too, after writing in his private notebook:

'But have I really got my father's imprint on my flesh and my spirit? I sometimes wonder, with terror.'

They all hated him. And suppose, now, suddenly, Malétras forced the young man to turn and look him in the face and said to him:

'Look at me. Look carefully at your uncle Malétras, whom you think you know. Yesterday at this time he was so unhappy, so miserable, that he squeezed a woman's neck with his big fingers, a child, like the girl your friend Jean wants to kill himself for. But he strangled her. Do you understand now?'

What could the boy understand?

Malétras suddenly realised that he would have to be careful. Thinking like that had been just a game, and now it was becoming a temptation. With Hermine earlier, in the boudoir—he didn't like to call it that—he had contented himself with thinking:

'What would she do if I told her. . .'

35

It had not gone any further. He had not really wanted to try it out.

Now, as he stood with one hand on the boy's shoulder while Philippe wrote with flushed cheeks, his breathing suddenly became heavier, as it did when he was overcome by certain desires, and he paused in his dictation.

'Suppose I said to him . . .'

The young man, no longer hearing his voice, half turned his head, surprised, and Malétras regained his composure

'. . . at the rate of one hundred francs per month.'

'Write the date and sign. Here are your five hundred francs. Now go.'

'Thank you, Uncle.'

'No.'

'What did you say?'

'I don't need your thanks.'

'All right. Shall I say goodnight to my aunt?'

'No need to disturb her. You can go. You know the way. Don't shut the door too hard.'

He had a horror of slamming doors.

He remained standing in his study; then he closed the copper inkstand, put the pen back in its place, and slipped the receipt into his wallet.

Suddenly he jumped. He seemed to have been standing there for some time when he heard a sliding sound on the parquet floor. Hermine had come in, with her glasses on, holding her pen.

'I wondered what you were doing. Has he been gone long? Did he want money?'

'Yes.'

'Did you give it to him?'

And as if he was ashamed, in front of her, of having given it, he exaggerated his stance, looked at her defiantly, and snapped:

'Why not?'

4

It was not yet two days since the event had occurred, and he found himself able to continue scrupulously keeping to the habits that, to him, had become absolute rules. It had been thirty-two hours, he calculated while shaving at half past five in the morning in front of the bathroom window, which faced the street. The new shoots of one of the young planes grew within scarcely two metres of him, and as he opened the window a cloud of birds flew away. They must have been used to this large man with cheeks covered by lather, his broad thighs bulging through his underpants; at any rate, they returned one after the other to their perches.

Some people get up early but begin the day half-dressed, in slippers, perspiring, with a clammy mouth. But when Malétras came downstairs at about the same time as Eugénie, he was already meticulously washed and dressed.

As usual, she was bent over the fire, which she never managed to light the first time. As usual, he remained standing in the kitchen watching her, and he could not help sighing. She knew he was just behind her. She could not stand his long silences and his sighs. She hated him.

'I shall never get used to an employer who comes down to the kitchen at six in the morning. The other gentleman got up early too, but he waited in the dining room until I sent in the breakfast with his batman.'

She was Hermine's servant. And she had been with her for more than twenty years. Although Malétras had brought part of the furniture and some silver and crockery to the new household, in terms of servants he had contributed nothing. Rose was new. Renée, who came to sew and mend three days a week, was Hermine's former dressmaker.

Eugénie went off angrily to fetch a can of fuel from the scullery. She must have been doing it on purpose, since it was forbidden, and Malétras's silent reproof irritated her.

'If you don't want me to use it, you had better change the flue, which doesn't draw. And what an idea, putting the kitchen in the basement!'

This was what she found most humiliating. The architect had installed the kitchen down there, and it was certainly roomy and very well arranged, but the window was at ground level, and old Eugénie could see only the feet and legs of passers-by.

'If I open the window for some air,' she claimed, 'I'm lucky if the dogs don't pee into my saucepans!'

'Did you keep the soup for me, Eugénie?'

'Don't worry. You won't waste away today. You'll get your soup.'

While she was warming it, even before making the coffee, Malétras opened the refrigerator, where there were always some leftovers for him, a chicken leg, a slice of pâté, a piece of sausage.

'When did we have the leg of mutton, Eugénie?'

'You can remember just as well as I can.'

'It was at least five days ago.'

'If you say so, you must think it's true.'

'What's this piece here?'

'Well, at least it's making you talk.'

'When were you thinking of giving it to us?'

'How should I know?'

He could not help it: he suffered whenever he saw food being wasted, and Eugénie had a habit of leaving leftovers around for days, until they had to be thrown away.

Perhaps he would have suffered more if he had not been able to quarrel with Eugénie every morning. She had no respect for him and would snap back at him, shrugging her shoulders, serving him with abrupt gestures.

'Do you really have to come and eat in my kitchen in order to poke your nose everywhere?'

'I'll eat where I please, Eugénie.'

'Yes, you eat where you're used to eating!'

Like a peasant, it was true. On the scrubbed wooden table, without a cloth. He had even bought himself a big flowered bowl, which reminded him of his childhood, to eat his soup out of in the morning. He was sorry sometimes that he could no longer pull a knife out of his pocket to cut the bread or meat in his hand.

What did Eugénie really think of him? He would like to know. She was one of the few people whose opinion interested him.

'What's the matter with you this morning, staring at me like

38

that? You're like a boy who's done something bad and wants to confess.'

In fact, he had just been thinking:

'If anyone ever suspects the truth, it'll be Eugénie!'

She was uneducated. She could hardly read or write. But she had the knack of guessing what people were up to, particularly those she did not like—Malétras, therefore, more than anyone else.

'Suppose I suddenly said to her: "Eugénie, I've killed a woman. . . ." What would she do? I bet she'd believe me. She's probably the only one who would. She wouldn't jump. She'd just say: "You're quite capable of it!" '

He continued eating, thinking along those lines.

'I wonder if Eugénie has ever suspected that I had another life outside home?'

'You'd better hurry up; otherwise the dog'll do his business in the hall again. You might as well make some use of getting up so early when you could stay in bed every day. I'm really sorry for the people who worked for you when you were the big boss!'

It was indeed time for the dog, a little yellowish mongrel with a chopped-off tail, which made him look like a sausage, but with eyes that Hermine thought enormously intelligent.

In the past, and for a large part of his life, when Malétras came down at six o'clock in the morning, bowler-hatted, with his first cigar between his teeth, he would first walk across a large court-yard cluttered with boxes, sacks, and barrels, and go into the stables.

He owned twelve large horses, with heavy brass-laden harnesses, for deliveries in town; with his hands in his pockets, he would watch them being groomed and check the portions of oats. The warehousemen arrived next, then the office staff. Malétras was always there before them, stern and powerful, with never a word or a welcoming glance. Just one gesture, when someone arrived a few minutes late: he would draw his large gold watch out of his pocket and gaze at it, winding it up.

Nowadays, soon after six in the morning he opened the door, and the yellow dog would rush outside just in time to lift its leg at the first tree, while the master shut the door behind him and waited.

They walked together in the sun. A window opened here and there. Servants came out dragging dustbins. He walked with his hands in his pockets, turning round sometimes to make sure that the dog was following him, until he reached a newspaper stand half an hour from his house, where he always bought the morning papers.

Nothing had changed. He was doing exactly the same that day. It would be the same on the following days.

Standing in the middle of the square, whose keeper had not yet buttoned up his jacket, he glanced through a local paper; it did not mention Lulu.

She would not be mentioned; Joseph had promised that. It did not matter how he had gone about it. It was no longer Malétras's business. He had given him ten thousand francs. He did not want to know what he had done with Lulu's body. He did not want to think about it.

At eight o'clock, he picked out a little key from his bunch, opened the letter box, got out the post, examined the envelopes, and put Hermine's letters on a tray in the hall.

All his life his days had been minutely regulated. It was not an idiosyncrasy. It was more a discipline. He needed to mark out the day, to divide passing time into compartments, and he was convinced that it was thanks to this care that he had retained his unshakable steadiness.

He had felt that very much the previous evening, when he left the Cintra. There had been a gap in his timetable. He did not know what to do with the hour and a half he normally spent in Lulu's room.

Chance had led him into a curious bistro where there was only one old lady, and, without having actually decided anything, he seemed to know that he would return there today and every day.

So the gap was closed.

He shut himself in his office, read his letters, answered a few of them, opened and closed some drawers. He heard Hermine ringing for Rose to bring her breakfast, then the sound of running water filling up her bath. He could also hear the sound of his neighbour the doctor's car starting.

Had Eugénie guessed something? Probably not. She always looked at him with the same surly, suspicious eye.

Would she be capable of denouncing him to the police?

Probably not! Who knows if there would even be any change at all in her attitude? She hated him so much! She thought him so vile that the news that he had killed a young girl could scarcely add to her hatred and scorn.

'Kiki! . . . Kiki! . . .'

Good! Hermine was dressed. She was about to come down. She was calling to her dog from the first-floor landing, talking to him in a silly language.

Malétras disliked dogs, especially little ones who could not bite or frighten people.

There! She was down, opened the door. He stood up.

'Good morning. Did you sleep well?'

She refused to call him Jules—she thought it such a ridiculous name. Nor could she call him 'dear' with ease. So she usually did not call him anything. If it was absolutely necessary, if he was upstairs or in another room, she would shout:

'Malétras!'

She looked fresh. She exuded health and stability. She had an even temper. But they had nothing to say to one another, and soon she went downstairs to give instructions in the kitchen.

It was time for the fish market. He lit a new cigar, crossed a large part of town, and went into the Poineau brothers' shop. They always jumped when he came in, as if caught doing something wrong. He worked as fiercely at this unimportant little business as if his whole fortune depended on it. He had taken up his old habits of having a pencil behind his ear, of never removing his bowler hat in offices or shops, of answering the telephone in a rough voice as soon as it rang:

'Malétras here!'

Nothing had changed. He took the tram home. He nearly always brought back a fish or some shellfish. He went down to the kitchen to put it in the refrigerator, which gave him a chance to exchange nasty looks with Eugénie.

The siesta. The Cintra. A hard glance at Emile, who, like a dog one has absent-mindedly stroked, had since Malétras's smile become attached to him. The waiter greeted him, almost wagging his tail, and felt it necessary to say:

'An Imperial, Monsieur Malétras?'

Then, with a wink, he brought the anchovy canapés, which Malétras pushed away.

He did not play cards. He had never played cards in his life, except a few evenings with Lulu and Joseph, but that seemed to have been in another life.

He sat down behind the players and watched, smoking his cigar in little puffs. He did not understand bridge at all. When people had offered to explain the game to him, he had refused.

Why did that fat Steuvels look at him in that enquiring manner?

41

People are like that. Just because one has spoken to them once, they think themselves privy to ones secrets, just as Emile thought himself privy to Malétras's affections because of a chance smile.

What did those four think of him? When he had given up his business, Doctor Verel had said:

'You're wrong! You'll see! In less than six months you'll have to go to a doctor.'

But he had not been to a doctor. He had got through by himself. He had never needed anybody in his life. He had taken up the Poineau business. Then there had been Lulu.

'At our age,' Verel said, 'one shouldn't suddenly change one's way of life, especially when it has been an active one.'

They played bridge for hours, regarding pieces of coloured card as a serious, even tragic, matter, endlessly discussing a bid of two diamonds or three no-trump.

All four, even Verel, who was the son of a postmistress in the country, had struggled to get where they were. Steuvels had been a delivery boy in a brewery before becoming a brewer himself. Devismes, who appeared so proper, so well bred, had been a woodcutter in Gabon.

And now?

They mostly had married or marriageable children and they came to play cards at the Cintra; they were thrilled to call Emile by his Christian name and have their table kept for them, a table no one was allowed to sit at after four in the afternoon.

Did they regard Malétras as part of their little circle? Not entirely. Sometimes they would hint at some story they would not tell in front of him. There were silences when he came in. They watched him when he went out.

What was the difference between him and them? Why, all his life, had there been the same difference between him and those he mixed with?

He looked at his watch. Even in front of a station's public clock, with its huge dial, he would look at his watch, in midwinter, too, when he had to unbutton his overcoat and his jacket in order to pull it out of his waistcoat pocket.

'Emile!'

Would Emile still rush forward so slavishly if he said to him out of the blue:

'By the way, I strangled a woman after I left here the day before yesterday.'

He had not once in the last forty-four hours thought about Lulu

42

herself. It never occurred to him to feel sorry for the poor girl, dead at nineteen, whose body was now God knows where.

He was certainly haunted by his crime, if one could thus interpret the fact that he was conscious all the time that something had happened that had changed his life.

But the major character of the tragedy was not Lulu. It was he. Lulu was just an accessory.

He had only an inkling of the real tragedy: that was the story of Jules Malétras, son of the postman at Steenvorde, on the Belgian frontier, who had married, had two children, founded the Malétras Docks and run them for thirty years by sheer hard work; a strong, stern man, stronger and tougher than anyone else he knew, and who now for months had been driven to go out every evening, hugging the walls, to meet a plain little girl in a disgusting room at the end of a stinking alley.

Then, because she did not want to undress that evening, because a little earlier she had gone out in a car with that well-dressed fool Laniel, Malétras had taken her by the neck and strangled her.

It was time. He had been right when he had predicted, the night before, and that same morning, that this would henceforth be the time. He had hardly left the Cintra, and yet he was already walking in streets full of life and sunshine, which cast a kind of spell on him.

The real weather and the bright colours of the crowds made no difference: he could smell winter smells, feel drizzle; he pictured pools of light beneath the gas lamps; he felt his black overcoat over his shoulders, the touch on his cheeks of the upturned collar and, almost unconsciously, found himself immersed in a poor quarter, threading his way through unfamiliar streets.

He stopped suddenly, annoyed because he had lost his way. He could not find the old lady's bistro. He had not taken the precaution of looking at the street name. Panic seized him at the thought that he would never again see that place, where all he had done was sit alone for half an hour.

'I came from the cross-street. I must have turned left. Then I soon got to the church. . . .'

He focused his mind on retracing last evening's route, and succeeded, recognising the open door and the noise of the gang of children playing in the middle of the street. Next door there was a cobbler's shop; he breathed in the smell.

He entered, as relieved as if it had been really important. And, as on the day before, the place, with its four tables and polished zinc counter, was empty. As on the day before too, the kitchen door opened and he heard the warbling of the canaries.

The old lady in slippers recognised him and smiled.

'Still just as hot, isn't it?' she said, slipping behind her counter.

It was cool inside the bistro. Malétras was already enjoying its particular sort of freshness. The sun touched the other side of the street but did not reach this side, where the paving stones gleamed as they had done in some of the places Malétras had lived as a child.

The sun touched the first floor opposite, lighting up a window decorated with geraniums as if with the thick stroke of a paintbrush.

'A little anisette?'

Did she understand that from now on habits must not be changed? She took a carafe and went through the kitchen. She could be heard pumping in the yard, and for a moment there was a draft; he could just see the edge of a well, and green moss between the paving stones, like something in the country.

Then she went to fetch her work, which was no longer a napkin to be mended, but a piece of pale-green knitting.

A boy of seven or eight, who had been playing in the street, came and parked himself on the doorstep, staring at the gentleman with unconcealed curiosity.

'Go away, Fernand!'

There were two little girls sitting on the other side of the street. One of them had a big pink ribbon in her hair, like a doll, and a long stream of mucus between her nose and her mouth.

The old woman said nothing. Malétras said nothing. He smoked his cigar, gazing blankly in front of him, and from time to time he or the woman would heave a sigh, as if to mark the passing of time. Noises could be heard, the shouts of women calling each other from one doorstep or window to another, children's names echoing up and down the street.

'Germaine! . . . Germaine! . . . Come back! . . . If I have to come and get you . . .'

The old lady examined her customer from head to foot with quick looks, furtive little glances immediately drawn back like a cat's claws; once or twice, she opened her mouth, as if about to speak, but reluctantly closed it again.

A shape appeared in the rectangle of the doorway. A long,

thin, dark girl, bareheaded and barelegged, peered into the shadows, and quickly started to go, murmuring:

'Sorry . . . you've got company. . . .'

'Come in, Martine. Come here a minute. I've got something for you.'

The girl, who must have lived in a nearby street, walked across the room, swaying her hips, excusing herself as she went past Malétras with a glance that was both curious and respectful.

'Come in. . . .'

They shut themselves in the kitchen; the glass door was covered by a lace curtain. Malétras heard them whispering for quite a while. The door opened.

'I'll let you know . . .' said the old lady, concluding their mysterious conversation.

'All right . . . Sorry, monsieur . . .'

She looked at him again, slightly more boldly this time, hopped down the two steps like a little girl, and went away.

The old lady sat down again, and it seemed that she was about to speak. She hesitated.

'She's very young, still just a child,' she finally murmured, with a gentle smile, as if she were speaking of a girl making her first communion.

Malétras did not answer, appeared not to have heard.

'She's just sixteen. . . . She sometimes comes to see me, just like that. . . . But she's shy. . . . When she saw that someone was here, she wanted to go away.'

The stange thing was that he still did not understand. He was thinking. What was he thinking about, after all? He sat there as if in a cool bath. He watched the reflections on the glasses and bottles, he breathed in the coarse, heavy smell, he listened to the noises and cries of the street.

'If you'd ever like a little girl like that . . .'

He started, like a man being awakened. The old lady, who had taken up her knitting, thought he was going to become angry and go away forever. She said to herself that she had gone too fast, or that she had been wrong. She wondered whether he might be from the police, but reassured herself at once because of the unmistakable details: the suit of fine cloth, the made-to-order shoes, which she had admired the day before, the linen, the watch and heavy gold chain.

'I'm just saying that, you know . . .'

45

He stared at her as if she were one of those objects one suddenly notices although it has been in front of one for a long time.

'It does happen that gentlemen like you, who don't want to be seen with women, and want to be quite undisturbed . . . It's none of my business, of course. You can just as well come here for a drink. . . . You mustn't get me wrong. . . . Little girls like Martine, with trouble at home, just come and say hello to me when they're passing.'

Her mind was obviously working hard, and she seemed not quite at ease; this silent customer remained an enigma to her.

Why had he come back if it wasn't for that? He was rich—you could see that. He was an orderly, serious man—that you could see too—with an orderly mind.

And yet she had scented something unmistakable, something furtive and shameful.

If it was not a vice, then what was it?

Unless it was just not that particular vice?

She smiled at him to put him at ease. She was afraid that he might leave.

'I must say that you're not the first respectable—yes, even important—gentleman to come and have a drink with old Maria. . . .'

The strange thing was that he too was suddenly afraid of no longer being accepted. Not of being thrown out, of course—he could not be thrown out—but of no longer being accepted into the intimacy of the bistro.

'Give me another drink,' he said. 'Have one yourself.'

'You're very kind. I won't say no. . . . I was afraid I'd annoyed you. There's no harm in it, is there? A man's a man. . . .'

She was wrong about him; she felt it. And yet, God knows, she had had plenty of experience with men, particularly this kind: rich, middle-aged, with a sober and comfortable life elsewhere—men who, in the common phrase, 'have everything they need at home.'

'Your health.'

'And yours.'

She felt sure that she had unwittingly made him realise something.

'There's no harm in it, is there?' she had said. 'A man's a man.'

No! He had not come here for that. He had no desire for the girl who had just come in, nor for any other.

46

To tell the truth, he had never desired Lulu physically. He had strangled her out of jealousy and yet he had not loved her.

Had he ever desired a woman? When he was a young man, his friends—what friends he had had—mocked him for still being a virgin at twenty.

It was not because he was virtuous. Or shy either. Or impotent. He was as capable of making love as the next person. Perhaps even more than most, since he was extremely strong.

Women did not interest him. They complicated life. He was shocked by the importance attached to such a banal activity.

He had married because at that time he was alone, living in a furnished room and, for the sake of economy, cooking his meals on a gas ring.

He worked for a trading house. He went to classes in accounting in the evening, but found time to do the bookkeeping for several small tradesmen after work.

He had met Louise, who worked in a sweet shop. She was beautiful; he knew that. Not pretty, but beautiful. She was serious. She lived with her mother and her sister, who was also a shopgirl.

Given that man must marry, he considered that she would make a suitable wife. Also, marriage would give him a more respectable image. Finally, if he was better cared for—and almost as cheaply—he would be able to work in better conditions.

Had he been unfaithful? Hardly! Later, two or three times, after dinners, friends had dragged him to brothels. He had tried, so as to be like the others, with more revulsion than pleasure, and had felt humiliated.

Once, once only, during one of his first wife's illnesses—more precisely, when she was giving birth to his daughter—he had made use of one of the salesgirls, a small dark girl who kept giving him bold looks and seemed to be laughing at him.

'There,' he seemed to say as he pushed her back onto his desk, after closing time. 'Happy now?'

He fired her a few days later, on the first possible pretext.

Louise had not been the wife he had hoped for. He should have been more careful. Ever since, he had had a horror of families with troubles.

'Poor, but honest . . .'

And people, women especially, with sensitive feelings. All her family, men and women, had sensitive feelings. They had known better days. The father, who was dead, had owned quite a large coal business. He was a drunk, and had ended up bankrupt.

47

As far as his brothers-in-law and sisters-in-law were concerned, he, Malétras, was a brute. He had no feelings. Louise was unhappy with such a person.

So unhappy that she began to drink!

'Like her father and brothers!' he had replied to them coarsely.

She stole bottles from the shop. When she was in town, she would, under the pretext of a call of nature, go into the first bistro she saw and drink a few little glassfuls.

She had died. He had met the general's widow. She was dignified and distinguished. He was bored living with his daughter, whom he did not get along with.

He had remarried. He had remarried exactly as he had had the house built on Rue de la Commanderie. Wife and house went together. He respected his wife. They got on well together. At night there was somebody next to him in case anything happened.

Now here was a woman like old Maria, who should have understood everything, getting him wrong. Suppose he spoke to her about Lulu? Suppose he said: 'I had a girlfriend, a waitress I picked up in a café, whom I used to visit every evening. I strangled her'? She would put the action down to passion, or depravity.

And the lawyer? If they found the body, held an enquiry, and little by little traced it to him, and arrested him?

The newspapers would say: 'A crime of passion.'

The lawyer would, in his defence, speak of the passion of a mature man, a man already in decline, for a girl who laughed at him and who . . .

The truth was that he had not made love to Lulu as many as five times that winter! The truth was that he could quite easily not have touched her. He hardly wanted to. It was of minor importance. In fact, it was she who had wanted . . .

And he had given in because she would not have understood, in much the same way as, when one sits down in a café, one has to have a drink, even if one is not the slightest bit thirsty.

Lulu thought of nothing else. She thought she was giving him pleasure. She was always half-undressed, displaying her body.

The first time, he remembered that, as she was noisily expressing some real or feigned pleasure, he had said harshly:

'Shut up.'

She had been amazed. She had looked at him, about to cry.

'Aren't I doing it the way you like it?'

What a question! He was clearheaded enough, surely, to know

that in these situations a fat man like himself was always ridiculous, not to say revolting.

Like that little girl earlier . . . He now understood the look
she had given him. She had hoped . . . And what had the two
of them been whispering behind the kitchen door?

'I don't know yet. . . . He's not saying anything. We must go
carefully. Don't get too far away. . . . I'll talk to him and then
I'll call you back. . . .'

He wondered if he would return to this place, even though he
had found his niche here and felt so comfortable.

'You see,' the old woman went on—she was avoiding dangerous
subjects now—'it's always cool in here, even in the greatest heat.
If necessary, I open the doors to the kitchen and the yard, and
that makes a draft. Are you going already?'

He had pulled his watch out of his waistcoat pocket and sprung
open the gold lid. It was not time yet. He leaned back a little and
relit his cigar, much to the old woman's satisfaction.

'If you want to do me a favour, you'll accept another round. . . .
Yes, mine! I insist!'

He accepted. A little later he saw the young girl pass by across
the street. He did not look at Maria; he felt sure that she was
making a sign to the girl that meant:

'No good. You can go.'

5

He was at the Cintra. As usual, he faced the card players. Glancing at the street, for no special reason, he recognised Joseph on
the opposite pavement, hurrying away.

Perhaps he was only passing. But Malétras was sure that when
he had looked towards him, the former waiter from the *Normandie*, with his neck stretched out, had been busy spying on him,
and that it was only when caught in the act that he had walked
away, betraying himself by his hurry.

This was the fourth day after Lulu's death. Instead of being
frightened, Malétras got up and walked to the door, hoping that

perhaps Joseph was waiting for him at the corner, but he could no longer see him.

He changed none of his habits, smoked his cigar, left the Cintra at the usual time, and made his way by a now familiar route to Maria's little bistro.

An idea had come into his head earlier, while he was walking Hermine's dog in the fresh, new-looking street. He was not thinking about anything in particular. It could hardly be said that he was thinking at all. Outside of business, he was not the kind of man who would patiently follow the thread of an idea from its beginning in order to discover what was at the other end.

Because he was, in effect, alone from morning to night, and if there were empty spaces in his timetable, he filled them, unconsciously, with what others might call daydreams.

For example, in the morning, when he went out with Kiki into the still-sleeping street, Eugénie's image always remained in his mind for some part of the way.

'It's true that she's like a dog who can only have one master. . . .'

Indeed, Eugénie, who was so ill-tempered with everybody, and with him in particular, truly worshipped 'Madame Hermine.'

She was furious because of the ham.

He had eaten some ham he had found in the refrigerator. Eugénie had told him that she had bought it the previous evening to fill some ravioli with.

'You can go and get more.'

He looked at the sparrows. . . . The sparrows reminded him of the schoolyard. . . . That memory brought with it another, not a precise one, a puff of air, a fresh draft through the hot and heavy atmosphere, birds flying out of the lime tree, he flying off as well in a clatter of clogs, with his satchel on his back. . . .

He pushed a door with transparent advertisements on it; a little bell rang and . . .

He stopped, surprised to have reached this point. The smell! There was, in the house where he was born and had spent the first twelve years of his life, a smell he had often, since, been on the point of recapturing. He would be in a street and would stop to sniff, turn towards a door, approach it, but it was never quite right; it was too spicy or too insipid, with either one element too many or one missing.

What had suddenly struck him as he walked the dog, far from his little bistro and not even thinking about it, was that the smell at old Maria's was almost exactly the smell of his early home.

50

He felt happy about it all day. Henceforth he would feel less humiliated when he went to sit in the corner of that squalid place.

'I was attracted by the smell, without realising it.'

They sold drinks in his childhood home too. It was not a real bistro, but there was a counter in the corner, as there are in so many houses in the country, especially in the North. A smell of beer and gin would waft from there into the whole house, stronger than the grocery smell. At Maria's there was no grocery but the smell was almost the same; perhaps there was a grocery next door? Not to the right—the cobbler's shop was there—but to the left? He felt pleased that it was time to go and find out.

His day had been the same as all other days. He had gone to Poineau's, where he had worked like a clerk, but through the noises, the sunshine, the different jobs, there had always come that smell. With it there had sometimes come the memory of his mother's thin face; and, more curiously, he had begun to discover a resemblance between his mother and Lulu.

No, not a resemblance; Lulu had none of his mother's features. The latter had been very thin, with a long face and small eyes that were always tired. She was so tired that one wondered how she remained standing, coming and going as she did all day. They would say:

'You should rest, Madeleine. . . .'

She would reply, with a smile:

'I'll have plenty of time to rest when I'm lying next to the church.'

The first few times he heard that sentence, the boy had not understood that it meant the graveyard, and when he had understood, he had cried.

Today, in the tram, around midday, as he went home from Poineau's, he had glimpsed the wall of the cemetery, the iron gate, the first tombstones that one could see from outside, and tears had come to his eyes, just as they had when he had understood the sentence.

The idea wandered slowly through his mind, taking unexpected turnings, disappearing in order to reappear in another form, like a stream that sometimes pursues its courses underground and then reappears in an unexpected place.

His emotion—it was hard to explain—was involved as much with Lulu as with his mother. He promised himself that he would think about it later, at Maria's. He did not feel that it was a oaorilogo.

51

On the way he thought about Joseph too. He turned round several times to make sure that he was not following. If Malétras had seen him in the crowd, he would have gone straight up to him, and he would have had the explanation that he had wrongly failed to demand on the first day.

That was a bad memory. That day, the day after the accident, he had not been himself. It had been physical. The proof that it was physical, like the result of a drinking session, was that he had slept until nine that morning.

God, how he had walked! Really, he had been afraid. He had wandered in areas he did not know, and the memory of them remained unpleasant and continued to humiliate him. It was Joseph who had led him along the quays by the cranes. He had done the deciding, the reassuring.

Now it would be different. The man had returned, as might have been expected. He would want to blackmail him. Malétras would speak clearly to him.

He felt happy just going into the little street where the bistro was. The houses that leant towards each other, the light, the smell, the children—it was all as familiar as a childhood memory, and he smiled almost triumphantly when he observed that there was indeed a grocery next door to Maria's place.

There were transparent advertisements on the door. There were jars of stale pink and green sweets. There were also, next to the packets of macaroni and chicory, a few old vegetables.

Perhaps it was his mother's shop in Steenvorde that had given him the idea, later, of creating the Malétras Docks.

Maria, happy too, rushed out of her kitchen.

'How nice of you to come and see me,' she said, as if he was no ordinary client, as if he was now coming to her house as a visitor.

And, without asking him anything, she poured a glass of anisette and went off with her carafe to get some water at the pump in the yard.

It was truly the smell of his home. Up on the wall behind the stovepipe was the same official notice with the regulations on the sale of drinks.

In the café where Lulu had worked when he met her, the smell had been different. So that was not what connected the two women, her and his mother, in his memory.

He was unable to discover what it was. His first wife, Louise, the one who had started drinking, had not resembled his mother in the least.

She too had certainly resigned herself to life, but with sighs, complaints, and tears.

At home, the drunkard had been his father. He did rounds of thirty kilometres a day on foot in the early days, when Malétras was still very small—he could remember it—then later on a bicycle. He drank small glasses of gin all along the way, and when he came back, his reddish moustaches would be soaked with alcohol; he spoke in a loud voice, made assertive gestures; if there were people in the bistro, one could hear him shouting louder than the others, sticking to his guns at any cost, quarrelling about nothing.

His wife never complained. She never said a word about him to her children. She did have other children. She had had eight of them. There must be five left, including Malétras, but they did not count. One of them became a carpenter and still lived in Steenvorde, a daughter had married a bicycle seller from Hazebrouck who did some smuggling, another boy worked for the railway.

'Here's some nice cool water, my dear sir.'

When there was a customer, his mother too would run and get cool water from the well and come back wiping her hands on her blue apron.

Louise had never understood why he did not help his brothers and sisters.

'Help them how? Why? If a man is a carpenter, that's because he's made to be a carpenter. If he hasn't set himself up on his own, it must be because he's not capable of working for himself. I would not be doing him a favour by giving him money to set himself up. Just as I would be doing Martin'—he was the railway worker—'a disservice too by giving him money: he would just spend it and then be confused when he no longer had any.'

He had said to them, as he had said to Louise's family:

'Come and see me if you like. But don't expect anything from me. Anyway, it's not a good idea for you to come too often, or to bring your children; it can only arouse envy.'

Why was he thinking about all this when he was still searching for the connection that had unconsciously arisen in his mind between Lulu and his mother?

He looked at the old woman, who had come to sit near him, one chair closer than usual; she respected his silence and did her knitting, looking at him with surreptitious glances from time to time.

Did she understand now?

'If you'd ever like a little girl . . .'

Malétras's thoughts meandered on. His eyes wandered over various images: a glass, a bottle, a piece of pavement with a little girl sitting on the edge, an open window adorned with a blood-red geranium. . . .

It reminded him of the hours he had spent in bed when he had broken his leg and had stayed stretched out all day with his eyes half closed, next to the window.

He did not hurry, and made no effort to summon up the images. He let them come to him. A certain caution was necessary, so as not to frighten them away, because then they vanished without ever having properly formed.

He had loved only his mother. No other woman in the world! His mother and one other as well, a man, a boy, rather, an adolescent, his son, who had died and whose terrible thoughts about him he had read.

That was all. In fact, it was probably because of his mother, or her memory, that he had never loved a woman; he had never found one who resembled her.

She was a country woman. She could not have been very intelligent. He could not judge that, because she had died when he was only twelve.

Why did she love him more than her other children? His father could not stand him, because he was different from everybody else. He kept to himself even then. But he would obviously leave the nest as soon as he was strong enough.

What had his mother said?

'You might become somebody, my poor Jules, but I fear you'll be unhappy all your life. You aim too high.'

Had she foreseen, could she have foreseen, that, after years and years of struggle, when he was wealthy, well known, a member of the Chamber of Commerce, decorated, with a brand-new private house in the most elegant part of town, and a well-born wife, he would be sneaking down narrow streets in the evenings to go and spend an hour or so with a common girl in a room that smelt of poverty?

And that he would take pleasure in passing himself off as a poor clerk?

Now that Lulu was dead, he had, without really intending it, landed here, in a shabby bistro, with an old woman who dragged herself around on fat dropsical legs.

He had not chosen this refuge. And yet he had come here, so he had to assume that some instinct had led him.

At the moment when he had entered for the first time, he could not have known that the smell would remind him of his childhood. He had not realised it for the first two days. He had made the discovery far away, walking the dog on Rue de la Commanderie.

Now he felt that more would come. He was over sixty. For more than sixty years, he had lived without wondering why he did this or that, or where he was going, or whether his actions had a meaning, and now, in the normal course of events, his life was over. If things happened as they should happen, he would be in prison, he would be tried, and even if he was condemned to only a few years of hard labour, he would never return to normal life.

'It looks like thunder,' the old lady decided to say.

She wondered whether to speak or keep quiet. She suspected that he would keep coming back, that something drew him irresistibly, but she could not yet guess what it was.

A pervert is easier to please because one knows what he wants.

He looked at her as if not seeing her. He was far away, both in time and in space. Suddenly his mind returned to Lulu's room, and at that same moment he spotted Joseph going past.

He nearly got up to call him. He would have liked the conversation they were going to have to take place here, but the old woman would hear everything, even if he sent her into her kitchen. For a second he thought:

'Since she offered me a girl, she must at least have a room upstairs. I could ask to go up there with Joseph.'

'Are you going already?'

'No.'

He had nearly gone, yes, to catch Joseph, but he knew that he would wait somewhere for him. He did not want to show impatience. He did not want to admit to himself that, despite everything, he was a bit frightened. Suppose there had been a hitch in Joseph's plan? If the police . . .

He drank a second anisette, and let a quarter of an hour go by, during which the old lady told him that she had been a beautiful woman in her day, that men in those days gave her as much money as she wanted, but that she was too good-hearted, and because of this good heart she was now reduced to keeping a miserable bistro.

'It's not that I've got many needs. I just want to put enough money aside to be sure that at the end, when I begin to collapse, they won't take me to a hospital.'

He listened to her. 'Perhaps,' she thought, 'that is what this man wants, stories.' She had known some people who came only to listen to her tell sordid stories.

'My, you get all kinds! There are all kinds of tastes in nature, aren't there? And I always say that one has no right to throw the first stone. You won't believe me, but last week one came in, a nicely turned out gentleman, not fifty, not more than forty perhaps, who insisted on it, with me. . . . Yes, my good sir! I couldn't help laughing. . . . I was laughing so much that he went away furious. . . .'

He went away too, but only because it was time. Instead of turning right to go home, he turned left, the way Joseph had gone, and when he reached the end of the street, he found him waiting.

He still looked like a humble office worker who had had troubles. His face was sad, and covered with spots. He waited, leaving it up to Malétras to speak or not, and Malétras went up to him.

'I'm not bothering you? I didn't want to go to your house, or write to you. So I said to myself that I'd let you see me and you could choose your moment to speak to me.'

They walked side by side, retracing their steps when they reached the edge of the network of little streets and were about to emerge into a main road. Malétras smoked a cigar. With his hands behind his back, he looked as though he was doing business with an inferior.

'You're already back from Nice?'

'I went and I sent the letter. When I was there, I did some thinking, and I realised that in our hurry we didn't think of everything.'

Malétras caught the 'we' with a look, and the other man seemed to correct himself humbly.

'I mean I. . . .'

'Well?'

'Suppose the landlady was surprised not to find Lulu around. . . . The chances are she wouldn't worry and would just rent the rooms immediately to somebody else. . . . Still, she might

56

mention it to a furnished-room agent. . . . They make their rounds almost every week. . . .

'I've often been seen with Lulu. . . . Everybody knew that I was, as it were, with her. . . .

'I thought they'd think I'd gone with her. . . . So when they see me, they'll ask me what's happened to Lulu. . . .

'Do you understand? And with one thing leading to another, they might get to the truth. . . .

'Me, I said to you right away, all I want is for you not to have any trouble. . . . I said to myself: "It would be wrong if this man who has always been so generous, and isn't responsible since Lulu drove him to the limit . . ." '

'What have you come to Le Havre for?'

'I went to the building, as if I knew nothing. . . . I used to go for days without setting foot there. Rarely, but it sometimes happened. I beat on the door. I made a noise on purpose. A sailor who was sleeping off his drink with a girl opened the door.

' "What are you doing here?" I asked him.

' "What about you? What right have you got to come and annoy us?"

' "I want Lulu."

' "What Lulu?"

'I shouted so much that the tenants in the front building looked out their windows.

' "Have you seen Lulu?" I shouted to them.

'Then I went to the owner, who lives in the building next door. I acted like an angry man whose woman has double-crossed him.

' "And her things? What did she do with her things? I hope she hasn't taken them, because . . ."

'You understand? Like that, I'm covered, and so are you.

'In a little while, not too soon, because she didn't really write home all that often, I'll send another letter from Nice or Marseilles. I'll let it be thought that I'm going—I mean it's Lulu who's supposed to be writing, you understand—that I'm going to make a long journey to Egypt, maybe, or South America. . . .'

'And you?' Malétras asked simply.

'What do you mean, me? I don't understand what you mean.'

'What are you planning to do?'

'Nothing . . . What could I do? . . . When I'm better, I'll go to the company and ask to go to sea again. . . . With me, it's the blood that's bad, and the sickness always comes in the skin.'

'Listen, Joseph. . . .'

'Yes, sir . . . I'm listening.'

'Good, because I'm only going to say it once. First, it's all the same to me whether I go to prison or not. You may not believe me, but it's the truth, and I may prove it to you. So I've got nothing to fear from you. Go this evening and tell the police everything you know, and when they come to my house, I'll be ready to go with them.'

'But, sir . . .' the other stammered, horrified.

'It's a fact. Another fact is that if they arrest me, they'll arrest you at the same time. I'm not asking you what you did with the body. . . .'

'I . . .'

'I don't want to know. As for blackmailing me . . .'

'I swear, Monsieur Malétras . . .'

'I tell you I won't be blackmailed. Let's get that settled once and for all. The other day I offered you a hundred thousand francs and you refused it. I don't like that. I have never accepted free services in my life, because they're the most expensive kind. You refused a hundred thousand francs thinking, no doubt, that you would get more out of me by pretending to be uninterested. . . .'

'You're a hard man.'

'I'm precise.'

'What could I do with a hundred thousand francs?'

'That's right. I understand perfectly. Once you had spent the hundred thousand francs, you'd find yourself in the same situation as before. . . .'

'That's not what I mean. . . .'

'All right. Let's say, since it's your idea and it's not a bad one, that you go and send another letter, and that after that, with Lulu supposedly in Egypt or elsewhere, you don't concern yourself with it any more. Therefore, you have no business in Le Havre.'

'I've got my family.'

'What do you mean?'

'I mean my family is here, my mother and my sister, who . . .'

'Do you support them?'

'I do sometimes give them . . .'

'What does your sister do?'

'She's a seamstress. . . . She's got bad blood like me, and . . .'

'How much do you need to disappear permanently?'

'I don't want to go away.'

'Say how much. Don't be afraid.'

'I don't want to contradict you, but I assure you . . .'

'Three hundred thousand?'

'I know that's very tempting for a poor boy like me who . . .'

'Agreed?'

'No, sir, I assure you. You're wrong about me. One can see that you don't know me. If Lulu was still there, she'd tell you . . .'

'Is it no?'

'You see, I can't just go away like that. . . . Later, I don't know. One never knows what might happen. Give me time to think. . . .'

'I'm just warning you that it's three hundred thousand, as I just said, or nothing at all.'

'Yes, sir.'

'So, nothing at all?'

'Yes, sir.'

'I'm warning you too that I don't want to keep finding you in my way.'

'I'll try to avoid you. Today, I assure you, it was because I wanted to tell you . . .'

'Good-bye.'

'You're leaving me like that? You're wrong, sir. . . . You'll realise later that you've been too hard on me. . . . I'm worth more than you think, and if you ever need me for anything . . .'

'I won't need you again.'

'I hope not. . . . But one never knows, does one? At the moment, I'm living above the Bar de la Marine. . . . Do you know where that is? The blue-painted front . . . If I'm not there, they'll always know where to find me. . . . And if they ask which Joseph you mean, say it's the Joseph from the *Normandie*. . . . Good night, sir.'

'Good night, Joseph.'

And a minute later, when he was alone Malétras was surprised that he had said those words quite naturally, without malice, with involuntary cordiality.

He nearly turned round to call Joseph back.

What was the point? Everything was all right like this.

Since he was late, he took the tram to go home, and finished his cigar on the platform, dreamily watching the houses go by.

6

It was a little after ten in the morning. The sun shone radiantly, as it did every day during that period. A street-spraying cart had just gone by, leaving a cool trail on the asphalt. At a sidewalk café a waiter wiped the marble tables edged with brass.

Why was Malétras to remember with such precision details to which he had previously paid no attention? Right down to the shoeshop whose door was open, the smell of leather that floated out to him, the salesgirl up a ladder, squeezed into a black coverall, who seemed to be juggling boxes . . .

Right next to it was a great white marble entrance, four or five marble steps, brass handrails, and then the doors of the bank beating the air like wings with the continual comings and goings.

It was his bank; he had nothing to do there that day. But he automatically glanced at the vestibule, where the latest rates were written on a blackboard. One face struck him, an almost white beard, a stooped and stealthy figure. Somebody sad, unhappy, who did not want to meet anyone, or talk about his troubles.

'Gancel!'

Gancel started, looked around him with the worried face of a man torn away from his thoughts, a man who knows that he can expect nothing good from a chance meeting.

He recognised Malétras, tried to smile, showing long yellow teeth, which gave his face a somewhat equine look.

'How are you?' asked Malétras; his pitiless gaze took stock of the changes that had taken place in his friend in a few months.

The other man answered with a resigned smile:

'So-so, as you can see.'

'Your son?'

'He's well, thank you.'

'Is he still at the Mont Revard?'

'How did you know?'

This man who had worn himself down so much in a short time, who was so enfeebled, showing traces of wear at every seam, like

60

an old suit, was the father of Jean, the friend Philippe had gone
to join with Malétras's five hundred francs.

The two men remained standing in front of the bank. They had
often met in the forty years they had known each other, but it
would never have occurred to them to to go into a bistro together
or to sit down and chat in the nearest sidewalk café.

How many people of his own class, equals, did Malétras address
as 'tu' ? He searched his memory, because he was struck by this.
Gancel, and no one else. Gancel was the only one he tutoyered,
and he had never really noticed it, this Gancel who now seemed
drained, extinguished, who smiled so as not to be pitied.

'Your wife?'

'Still the same. How did you know my son . . .'

'From my nephew Philippe. Did you know that he has gone to
join your son in Savoy?'

'Jean told me that in a letter I received this morning.'

'And . . . what's he going to do?'

'You know about it?'

It was also curious that this man he called 'tu' was, of all those
he knew, the one whose character was most opposite his own.

They had been hardly more than twenty when they met.
Malétras was thin then, unlikely though that might now seem.
Gancel already had that square beard, always very well trimmed,
in the shape of a pack of cards and, at that time, pale blond.

He worked for a grain broker, while Malétras was employed,
a hundred metres away, by a wholesale grocer.

It was at the time when employees in trade gathered to plan an
association that would protect their interests. The meetings were
held on the first floor of a café that no longer existed, where there
were several billiard tables lit by batswing gas burners. There was
a smell of gas, which Malétras recalled when he looked at Gancel.

Gancel had been named treasurer of the association, which had
never had any funds and was to be short-lived anyway. He was,
already, the upright type that people asked to be treasurer. He
went to church each morning before going to work. On Sundays
he looked after children from a church children's club and he
could be seen, taking himself very seriously, blowing his whistle
to control a stampede of small children.

They were then at the beginning of life, and now they met again
at the other end. They had never lost sight of one another. It was
odd, because they had not done so on purpose. They did not
particularly like each other.

Later they had both set up up their own businesses, Gancel in cafés, Malétras with his docks. Malétras had often bought cafés from Gancel. Then, one fine day, they had found themselves, somewhere between forty-five and fifty, on the same board of directors—of that very bank outside which they were now standing.

'I think they will get married,' sighed Gancel, with a martyred expression.

'This girl appears to me to be everything that's most undesirable.'

Malétras was being savage on purpose. He had been Lulu's lover. For the last eight days of their liaison, until the moment he killed her, he had considered himself to be the most despicable of men, tolerating Joseph, ready to tolerate other lovers if necessary, lying to everybody, using childish tricks to spend money without his wife's knowing, and, finally, white with shame, speaking to someone like Steuvels, begging for the famous telephone call that would give him a few hours of freedom.

Well, Gancel, who had always been good and honest, who had always wanted to be good and honest, had sunk even lower than he had.

They must be the same age, give or take a year. Six months earlier, they still looked it even though Gancel's beard was completely white. Now there seemed to be ten years between them, because in one was apparent that collapse of the features which indicates approaching breakdown.

Soon, men of the same age, members of the same boards, rich businessmen like Steuvels, Legrand-Beaujon, or Devismes following a funeral cortege would say:

'He wasn't really old. It's amazing how quickly he went.'

Gancel was already half dead. Although his business had prospered and he had become very wealthy, he had suffered every possible unhappiness in his family life. His wife had been bedridden for fifteen years with an incurable illness. She had to be looked after, washed and fed like a baby, and every day she prayed to God to take her to Him.

His daughter was lame and had ugly features; she refused to get married, because she knew that a man would marry her only for her money. For fear of being smiled at, she dressed like an old woman and rushed to all the masses.

And now his son . . .

This in fact was Job standing before Malétras; he examined him curiously, without shame, without bothering to express compassion he did not feel.

'I went to ask advice from Father Clouet, who is my spiritual guide.'

'And what did Father Clouet say? This girl has had lovers, I gather.'

'Fewer than Mary Magdalene, anyway.'

Was he a true, sincere believer, without any reservations? In the past, Malétras had sometimes mocked him, because he ostentatiously displayed his faith, defying the laughter of unbelievers.

'Are you a Christian from the bottom of your heart?' he had asked him one morning like this as they emerged from a board meeting.

'I am a Christian.'

'You believe in the Gospels?'

'I believe in them.'

'In that case, I don't understand how you could have become rich. Because, in order to become rich, you and I have both had to stamp a few people underfoot, haven't we? You don't amass millions by practising humility and Christian charity.'

He could no longer remember what Gancel had answered. But whenever a new disaster befell him, Gancel went to his confessor for advice.

'I went to see the girl several times. She confessed to me that she is expecting a child. She claims, and it appears to be true, that the child is Jean's. She really loves him—I don't think one can put on an act to that extent.'

'So you're going to bring back your son and marry them?'

It was in the mountains that Malétras's son had died. Jean Gancel would live, he would live with a woman whom he could take nowhere—who would put an end to any future he might have.

'Is she pretty?'

'She's not beautiful. She's ordinary. She's not elegant, and her health isn't good.'

Like Lulu. So a young man of twenty-two had, like himself, found total pleasure in going to a miserable room to visit a girl who held no attraction for anyone.

'Have you written to your son to tell him your decision?'

'Not yet. I'll probably go to the Mont Revard myself, if my wife's health allows it. I shall speak to him man to man, not as

63

his father, but as his friend and elder. And if I feel that it is his fate . . .'

He too had been through forty years of effort, like Malétras! Forty years of pitiless struggle, because, as he had said before, you don't reach the point they had by taking pity on people.

There they both were, face to face, over sixty, in front of the bank where they kept their money, and where the employees rushed to greet them when they came in. In the street, people they hardly knew would respectfully salute the important citizens they had become.

'So this is what we've come to!' grunted Malétras, in conclusion to his thoughts.

Gancel did not understand.

'Your daughter?'

'I suppose she's well. I don't see her now that I've remarried. She still lives with her fool of a husband—he's already given her three children.'

'Is your wife well?'

'She's well, thank you.'

Once again, and this time more powerfully than ever, he wanted to say, in a perfectly natural voice:

'As for me, I strangled a girl. The sort of girl, indeed, that your son is going to marry!'

How would a Gancel react? And yet it was true—though it did not prevent him from standing in the street by a shoeshop and a bank, watching the yellow trams go by in the sun; it did not prevent him from taking little puffs on his cigar, or from enjoying the warmth of the air.

Of the two, Gancel was the most unhappy. He would return to a huge sad house, which smelt of illness and prayers, and would soon smell of candles and chrysanthemums.

'Good-bye,' he said abruptly.

And he went to Poineau's, looking forward to the time he would spend in Maria's bistro at the end of the day. On his way there, he happened to think about Joseph, but without disgust or fear. The day before, he had tried to get rid of him permanently, and now he wanted to see him, talk to him, question him.

The Poineau brothers greeted him as usual, with embarrassment and humility. These two giants, heaving crates of fish and lobster, suffered each morning when Malétras came into their place as the boss and talked to them as if they were ordinary workers.

Especially because Malétras waited until there were other people there to find fault and make disagreeable remarks.

It was his right, wasn't it? It was his money that was at stake; he had saved them from bankruptcy.

He went home on the tram. For the last few days, the dining-room door had been open at lunchtime, and the garden could be seen in full bloom.

Hermine, her lips in a thin line, seemed to be looking at him more carefully than usual, with a certain irony, which made him uneasy. She was silent throughout the meal, dropping, one after the other, conversations he tried to start. Only when the coffee had been brought in did she murmur casually:

'Tell me, my dear . . .'

That was a bad sign, because the few times she called him 'my dear' she had something unpleasant to say to him.

'Do you remember that evening last week, when you had dinner with your friend Steuvels?'

He had rarely blushed in his whole life. He did not have much colour; his complexion was pale, if anything. But he felt his ears burning.

'Well?'

'Did you dine at Steuvels's house?'

'You know I didn't. If the dinner had been at Steuvels's house, you would have been invited, or else I wouldn't have gone.'

'Was your friend Steuvels in good spirits that evening? Did he say anything special?'

He pretended to search his memory.

'Special? . . . No . . . I don't see . . .'

'Did he talk to you a lot?'

'Could you tell me what these questions are all about?'

At a moment like this he hated her—just because of those qualities that had driven him to marry her: that calm, that dignity, that well-bred elegance that had so impressed him.

Was it her birth, her education, or the fact that she had been the wife of a general that made her feel so superior to him?

He felt furious and humiliated. He got up and drew a cigar from his case.

'When you tell me frankly what you're driving at, I shall answer.'

'Well! I am sure that your friend Steuvels dined at home that evening.'

He said, sarcastically:

'Really! He told you that?'

Because she knew Steuvels, she might have met him in town; and Steuvels was quite stupid or nasty enough to have given himself away, as if by accident.

She went on, without answering his question, more sarcastic than before:

'I can give you his menu for that evening. They had a nephew to dinner, a nephew from Antwerp who arrived unexpectedly. They had nothing special in the house, so the cook rushed all over town to find some live lobsters. She unearthed some, despite the late hour, and cooked them *à l'américaine*.'

'I'm delighted to hear that, but since I didn't dine at their house, I didn't have any.'

'Steuvels did. He even made a scene with the cook because she put in too much red pepper. You see how well informed I am.'

'If you interrogate our friends' cooks!'

'Don't worry, my dear. Just tell me frankly, instead of behaving like an obstinate child, who you dined with that night, with such abandon that you came home drunk.'

'With Steuvels.'

'Still? Shall we telephone him?'

'If you insist.'

'The telephone is next to you. Ask for the number.'

He nearly did, out of bravado. This scene was ridiculous, and of the two he felt the most ridiculous.

'I don't want to make you suffer any more.'

'Me?'

'Yes, you, my poor fellow—or put you in a humiliating situation. Would you believe that Eugénie . . .'

'You might have warned me that it was your cook's gossip.'

'Eugénie, whom you love so much, and who returns your affection, met the Steuvels's cook, who is a friend of hers, this morning at the market. They were talking about this and that and they ended up on the subject of the dinner and Steuvels's temper.'

'And of course Eugénie couldn't wait to come and tell you.'

'Of course.'

'Do you believe her?'

'I've never had any reason not to, since she has never lied to me.'

'Thank you.'

'You're welcome. Whom did you dine with?'

'With friends.'

'You got Steuvels to ring me up just to have dinner with friends?'

'You said yourself that his nephew arrived at the last minute. He was going to come with us, and then he sent a message. . . .'

'It's a pity you go on lying. Although I must say that it's all the same to me. I'm not jealous. At the moment, I'm more concerned with you and my dignity.'

'What dignity?'

'Don't you understand? You might as well know that you've been seen with her.'

Now he began to be really frightened, and kept quite still in order not to betray himself.

'It's still Eugénie who . . .'

'It's still Eugénie, yes. You'll see how chance arranges things. She always gets her eggs and cheese from the little dairy at the corner. The shopkeeper has a twenty-year-old son who's rather worthless. You don't know him, but he knows you. The whole quarter knows the important Monsieur Malétras, at least by sight. . . .'

'I still don't understand.'

'This son sometimes frequents those bistros of ill repute around the docks. Now who do you think he chanced to meet in one of these places? None other than the great Monsieur Malétras we just mentioned. So you know how to play cards and you never told me! And I've often asked you to invite friends in to play bridge. My poor man, how I pity you!'

'Is that all you have to say?'

'Don't you think it's enough? Don't you understand how pathetic it is for a man of your age and position to go and exhibit himself with a grubby little girl in God knows what little bistros? The whole street knows about it. You were playing *belote*! And gazing at her! Apparently you were like a poor fat doggie waiting for a piece of sugar! She calls you "tu"! She drives you along like the poor fool you are, and you, you fawn on her. . . .'

She changed her tone abruptly and became serious, hard even.

'Do you intend to continue this relationship?'

He looked at her without answering, and his eyes were full of hatred.

'I asked you a question. I want to know if you intend to go on running after street girls.'

'Why?'

67

It was his turn to repeat himself, threateningly, when she remained silent.

'Why?'

She turned about and went towards the door, saying merely: 'You'll see!'

She left. He heard her going up to the next floor. A few minutes later she came down, and the front door opened and then closed.

No doubt she had just gone to do some shopping in town, or to see a friend—she had kept her own friends.

He was worried all the same. He had imagined many possibilities, including the real catastrophe. And the prospect of prison had hardly frightened him.

But now he had been hit, not by any precise accusation, but by the gossip of shops and servants' quarters. He had been seen with Lulu! He had been seen playing cards in one of those dives he sometimes used to go to with her and Joseph.

And Hermine was jealous!

Jealous of Lulu, who was dead!

He hit the table so hard with his fist that it hurt, and, leaving the dining room, where his coffee was growing cold, he went and shut himself in his study.

Jealous!

It was the most unexpected, the most staggering thing. They did not love one another. They had never had the bad taste to talk about love. It had never occurred to Malétras to kiss Hermine on the mouth.

They had married because they were old. That was the harsh truth. He had made the mistake of giving up his business at an age when he was still too active to remain idle. He had never been so bored in his life as in his daughter's pretty villa, where he had lived for more than a year.

It had never occurred to him that one might live alone. He could not see himself in furnished lodgings or an apartment, like a pensioner.

He had wanted a house, first, and it was because of the house that he had thought of a wife.

There was no love on either side. She was a widow and he was a widower. They had both lived. They were reaching the age when you suffer from various disabilities, when you take care of yourself, when sometimes in the night you feel you are choking, your heart beating too fast, and you are seized with panic.

During the day they were like people who are acquainted, not more than that, people who might, for example, have lived for a long time in the same hotel. They said 'vous' to each other. They exchanged civilities like strangers. They talked about their business affairs.

At night they undressed in the same room, without modesty, showing their aging bodies; sometimes they would attend to one another's needs.

Hermine was jealous!

They both had a few years left to live. Had Malétras had too much happiness until then? Had he not worked like a slave? If pleasure offered itself, surely it was allowable that . . .

The truth was not what she thought; she took him for a dirty old man who chased little girls.

Well! Even if that were true? By what right could she refuse him these last pleasures?

He had not always been an atheist. In the past, in his adolescence, he had been part of a Catholic group, because he had thought that one could be helped by priests.

He had studied the Bible and the Scriptures. He remembered a passage, which he had not understood at the time, and had taken for some sort of anomaly, the passage about David, the holy man, calling for young virgins to warm his old man's bed.

There were two of them in this big sunny, opulent house, two almost at the end of their lives, two who had come together only to live out their last years as best they could, and now Hermine . . .

He knew her. Once such an idea was in her head, she would always look at him coldly, with curiosity mingled with disgust.

It was the end of their tranquility, of the care they showed for one another in little ways.

Had his daughter not behaved in much the same way? He had given her everything. As a little girl she had been the most spoilt child in the whole town. He had made a point of honour of refusing her nothing. But, God knows, she had a bad character and treated her father harshly!

He had given her a large dowry. He had accepted the idiot of a husband she had chosen because he was elegant and part of a smart circle.

He had built her one of the prettiest villas between Caen and Deauville.

And he had given his son-in-law, who wanted at least to appear to work, the necessary funds to buy an interest in a garage.

69

Had he not the right, having behaved like this, to live the rest of his life as he pleased?

Clearly not. As soon as he had spoken of remarrying, there had been, first, tears, then threats.

'When I think of poor Mother in her grave . . .'

As it happened, this same crying girl had in the past cold-bloodedly locked her mother in a storeroom when her little friends came to visit her, because she was afraid that they might see that she drank.

She had beaten her once, beaten her almost to a jelly!

Her father wanted to remarry and she went to all kinds of lawyers, right up to the courts, in sickening pursuit of her own interests.

She and Hermine were worthy of one another.

He was alone, going round and round in his study like an angry bull. Even his son, the son who had been a god to him, the son for whom, without exaggerating, he would have unhesitatingly shed his own blood—that same son suffered, romantically, from having such a father, and confided these sufferings to a notebook!

Suddenly, just when he was least thinking about it, phrases from the conversation that had just taken place formed themselves into images: the little bistro that Hermine despised so much, the game of cards on a sticky advertising cloth bathed in reddish light.

. . . It was drizzling outside. They went out into the dark leaning forward, and Lulu quite naturally took his arm. . . .

. . . He went back with her to her room; there was no electricity, and she would lift the glass dome of the lamp, while he struck a match. . . .

What was happening to him? What was he staring at as he stood by the old desk that had followed him throughout his career? Not at the portrait on the mantelpiece, two children leaning towards each other in a pose arranged by the photographers—his son and daughter when they were three and five years old.

His eyes were open, but he could see nothing. He felt a strange heat in his eyes; they were clouding over, his lip was raised in a pout he had not experienced since his earliest childhood.

He could feel that he, Malétras, was crying. And instead of hiding his face, he went and leaned up towards the mirror without wiping his eyes.

It was not a pretty sight. An old man crying. An old man who suddenly collapses pitifully, and, failing to find sympathy around

70

him, looks with pity at his old head, watches himself in the cloudy depths of a mirror, crying alone.

He stammered:

'Lulu!'

What would he not have given now to go stumbling up the broken stone stairway at the end of the yard, above the carpenter's shop, to find her flopping on the bed, half-naked, in her dressing gown, to hear her say in her always slightly hoarse voice—she smoked from morning to night, reading her simple books:

'Have you brought me some chocolates?'

She was dead, just because she had wanted to go off in a beautiful sports car, because, all excited by the violent fun, she had answered his questions rudely, and refused to take her clothes off.

There was no other reason. She had refused to undress, although she was normally totally immodest, and would open the door to the postman or anyone else with her dressing gown half open, her breasts hanging out, her stomach naked.

She was thin. She had very white skin, slightly yellow beneath the breasts.

That evening, stupidly, like an obstinate child, she had not wanted to undress, and now she was dead.

He stayed with his elbows on the mantelpiece, his head in his hands, and went on crying; he was doing it on purpose, working himself up by crying.

Somebody was knocking at the door. He did not hear. They were trying to open it.

'Are you there, monsieur?' came Rose's voice.

He remained silent and guessed that she was getting worried. She was talking to somebody.

'But the door is shut from the inside.'

He made an effort.

'What is it?'

'A telegram.'

He took it through a chink in the door, without showing himself.

ARRIVED IN TIME AT MONT REVARD STOP WAS ABLE TO PREVENT THE WORST STOP HOPE ALL WILL BE WELL STOP MUST EXPRESS MY GRATITUDE AND AFFECTION STOP PHILIPPE

He looked around him, placed the blue paper on his desk, and, not knowing what to do, unable to recapture either his tears or

the image of Lulu, he stood as though empty of thought, and
sighed.

'Poor fool!'

7

It was not premeditated. And yet he instinctively chose areas and
streets whose appearance was most liable to infuriate or depress
him. He craved misery or anger.

It was just before nine o'clock at night; he was never normally
outside at this time, which was when dinner came to an end on
Rue de la Commanderie.

Malétras hated all deviation from rules. Ever since school, and
throughout his life, he had stuck scrupulously to timetables,
perhaps because he had little confidence in his own will power.
Moreover, he had always been afraid of that slate-coloured hour
that marks the transition between day and night.

He liked mornings, damp grey dawns; whereas twilight, with
its awful depth, was to him like a lake one might drown in, or a
desert one might lose oneself in. Or a night that was not
completely dark and might never end, rather the way his childhood catechism had described limbo.

In the centre of town he would still have found some activity,
men to rub shoulders with, familiar sounds. But he would inevit-
ably have gone from the centre towards old Maria's little street,
and he did not want to go there.

He plunged into the middle-class districts, with their wide,
gloomy grey streets; there was not a cat in sight, or, rather, not
a man walking. Sometimes a cat slipped from one door to another;
worse, there might be a concierge and her husband in shirt sleeves,
sitting on chairs in eternal poses.

Lamps were going on behind curtains. It was no longer light
enough indoors. Some people, with the window open, leaned on
the frontier of the night, emerging from an invisible world, quite
still too, as if it was a moment that forbad speech or noise.

A little earlier, he had suddenly fled from the silence in his own home. It had gone on for two days, since that stupid scene of Hermine's.

She had not spoken to him since then. Or, rather, what was worse, what emphasised the fact that her silence was wilful and permanent, she spoke just a few necessary words in his presence and avoided looking at him. This was what this woman, who thought herself superior, had discovered: he had cheated like a schoolboy in order to get himself a free evening; he had been seen playing *belote* in a little bistro at the port.

So, since he would not explain himself, she would henceforth remain silent. They lived in the same house, slept in the same bed, nightshirt to nightshirt, flesh to flesh, their smells mingled, but as far as any human contact went, any exchange of thoughts, it was all over.

She did not bother to appear sad, or in a bad temper. On the contrary. During dinner, for example, she kept calling Rose, on purpose, more often than was necessary, to chat with her.

'Rose, you must start thinking about your holiday. Tell me, where you are thinking of going this year?'

'Home, madame.'

And so on and so on.

Malétras felt crushed by a mountain of stupidity and spite, and suddenly, just as the dessert was being served, he got up, left the dining room, took his hat from the stand, and crossed the threshold.

He did not know where he was going, or when he would return. Embittered, he plunged sourly into these hateful streets, into this inhuman evening silence, which filled his heart with anguish.

At a certain moment he realised that he was not more than two hundred metres from Gancel's house. There was a street where he could have turned left or right, but he continued to walk straight on, knowing, or guessing, that, despite the odd hour, he would not be able to resist his confused urge to ring his friend's doorbell.

One does not call on people at nine o'clock in the evening without an invitation. He had set foot in Gancel's house possibly twice before, the last time being ten years earlier on an occasion he could no longer remember.

Even less should one call unexpectedly on a tired man whose wife is ill.

He lied to himself:

'I won't ring.'

Then he saw the huge dismal house, completely dark except for a window on the first floor. Even that had to be examined closely in order to see some yellow glow behind the thick curtains. And the bedrooms were on the first floor.

He rang, conscious of committing an aggressive act. He waited for quite a while before hearing the sound of a window being opened on the first floor; he looked up and saw Gancel's face sticking out.

Neither had time to say anything, because the door opened and a thin maid showed Malétras into a huge unlit hall, where she moved the light switch.

'Come in. I'll see if monsieur is here.'

She opened another double door, into a drawing room, freezing despite the season, where no life seemed to have penetrated for a long time, giving the impression that one was disturbing the privacy of its frozen contents.

Gancel came down, in slippers, slowly, because he was buttoning his detachable collar as he descended.

'Good evening, Malétras. I wondered who it could be.'

'I was passing. I thought I'd come in and say hello.'

He was disturbing them; that was clear. Gancel hesitated. It was impossible to receive a visitor, even an unwelcome one, in this drawing room, where the blinds had not been raised for months and green dust sheets covered the furniture.

'Come up for a minute. My wife will be pleased to see you. She gets so few visits!'

He did not dare send Malétras away.

'Do you mind if I go up for a moment to warn her?'

He still hoped for a refusal, but Malétras said nothing, remained heavily present. He knew that up there they were expecting him to come, because someone was quickly going to and fro, no doubt tidying the room. When old Gancel went up, the comings and goings became even more frantic.

What were they removing from sight? Those intimate, squalid things that lie about in sick-rooms? He recognised the particular sound of an enamel bucket being picked up by its handle.

'Come up, Malétras.'

Gancel called him from halfway up the stairs. Was it out of politeness that he showed no annoyance? Was it goodness, Christian charity? It was an old house, and its smallest details had taken on a permanent and solemn aspect, as if it were a presbytery or a sacristy.

'Come in. Give me your hat. I'm sorry to have to receive you here, but it's more or less the only room we use. You must understand. It's Malétras, Isabelle.'

The poetically named Isabelle was his wife; she lay on a sofa between the two windows, her body covered by a dark blanket. Everything was dark, the wallpaper, the old furniture, the shapes of people. Only the faces were light.

She said, in the faraway voice of a sick person already cut off from the living by a sort of veil:

'Sit down, Monsieur Malétras. My husband has so often spoken to me about you. You came once, I think, a long time ago, when he had tonsillitis, and you had to get him to sign some papers. Do you remember, Gérard?'

She smiled weakly.

'Alice, you should offer Monsieur Malétras something. . . .'

And their daughter emerged from the darkness, dressed in black, with black hair and black eyes. She had coarse and graceless features, more like a man's than a young girl's.

'What shall I get, Papa?'

This deformed creature had a very gentle, caressing voice.

They were rich, richer perhaps than Malétras, but they retained the modest habits of their early days.

'Go and get the little carafe in the dining-room sideboard. I think it is still half full.'

The house was huge, because that was the way they had found it, but they inhabited only a small corner of it; they had withdrawn to this sick-room, and it had gradually become their living room.

It was not meanness. They did not ring for the maid. Alice limped down the staircase herself.

Malétras knew what an imposition his presence was. What had he come for? Nothing. Or, rather, yes—he had come to do something precise, and the way he looked around betrayed him.

He had come . . . It was hard to say. . . . It was evil. . . . No, it was more merely shabby and low. It was worse than evil, because evilness implies a certain grandeur.

He had come to see people he hoped were more miserable than he was!

He and Gancel had started life together. They had worked and made their fortunes at the same time. They had married and had children, a boy and a girl each.

Two days earlier, he had, by chance, outside the bank, met a Gancel who appeared to have one foot in the grave already and

75

this evening, feeling a rising tide of rage and bitterness within him, he had been tempted to come and sniff around the misery of others.

'Is your wife well?'

'Very well. At least an hour ago . . .'

'You can see. Mine is fighting. She still suffers a lot but won't complain.'

'Everybody is so kind to me,' she murmured, her face assuming what is commonly described as a holy look.

'No, no. We're happy near her, you see? Anywhere else in the house seems empty. So little by little we've completely installed ourselves here. Right down to the desk I've put in the corner. We eat in this room. . . .'

That was why, despite the darkness, the room was redolent of warmth and intimacy. Everywhere, objects laid aside for a moment betrayed their owner's occupation: Gancel's book and spectacles by his armchair, some needlework by the girl's seat.

'I read out loud in the evening. My wife's eyes are too weak to read.'

Why did this not produce a feeling of boredom or great sadness? She was helpless and in pain for more than half the day and night. Gancel had been affected by his son's future taking such an unexpected direction, quite contrary to the traditions of the family, and was sapped—you could see it on his face—by an illness that would soon get the better of him. Alice, with a name as gentle as her mother's, ugly and unfortunate Alice, would in a few years, a few months even, be a lonely old maid.

Yet one could find no trace of hatred or revolt in any of their faces.

Only Alice's eyes, as she brought in a tray and some glasses, betrayed her feelings—mistrust of and anger towards the obtrusive visitor.

'Gérard speaks so often to us about you that we feel we know you very well,' said Madame Gancel.

The girl's eyes, on the other hand, said:

'We do not like you. You are a hard and wicked man. You didn't come here this evening by chance, and your motive can only be treacherous. What have you come to do to my poor father?'

At the next moment she gazed at her father, and her face was transformed; the adoration was painful to watch: surely no human being could feel such love for another, a daughter could not

76

harbour such a complete passion for her father, a little man with a white beard, broken by worry and old age.

'You'll have a little brandy, won't you? I don't know if it's good; we never drink it.'

When Malétras was a young married man, he too had had in his house, in the sideboard, a carafe of very commonplace alcohol, bought in small quantities from the grocer, which was offered, in minute glasses, only to unexpected visitors.

Were they waiting for him to give an explanation for his visit? He had none to give. He was not ill-pleased at inflicting on all three the torment of wondering what he had come for.

He was not contributing to the conversation, as he should have done. He sat there, heavily, with his legs apart and his glass in his hand; it was up to them to find something to say to prevent this silence, which embarrassed them more than him, from becoming more oppressive.

What had he come for? To see Job on his pile of manure. To see, in his own home, in the ugliness of his private life, a man who had every reason to complain about fate.

And yet this man, who had not much longer to live, was like a lover, full of care and attention for the emaciated woman stretched out beneath a blanket. He kept asking her silly little questions:

'Is there too much light?' 'Do you want me to turn the couch a little?' 'You're not too hot?'

And she looked at him with the same tenderness, the same trust.

That was what infuriated him: the trust all three had in one another. They could have lived forever, all day every day, the three of them in that room, sharing their unhappiness, almost unaware of it.

Malétras searched for a crack. He would have given a lot to find it, to discover one of those revealing little details, hairline cracks that suddenly reveal the harsh truth beneath the surface harmony.

'I had news of your son, indirectly.'

Surely this was the soft spot! Could he not at last upset them by pretending to put his foot in it? Alice certainly gave him her harshest look so far. Gancel, on the other hand, turned towards his wife to make sure the shock did not upset her.

'On the day we met . . . That afternoon I received a telegram from my nephew, Philippe, who went to join your son at the Mont Revard. . . .'

Then Madame Gancel murmured gently:

'Jean is very well, isn't he? He knows that his father would never do anything to hurt him. This girl seems to have a heart, and that's the most important thing in life.'

Alice proved that she had been watching him; in the face of Malétras's discomfiture she could not prevent herself from smiling, with both irony and scorn.

'I did what I had to do,' Gancel said, sighing. He put on his glasses after carefully wiping them with a piece of chamois. 'As for the rest, God will decide.'

Malétras shuddered. And his shudder reminded him of his years of catechism, when he was taught that the the Devil fled at the touch of holy water or the sight of a sign of the cross.

Holy water had just been thrown at him. He was the Devil. Being that and hating them all gave him a strange satisfaction.

His mouth was filled with bitterness—spleen, his priest would have said.

It gave him more satisfaction to see, in another, spite similar to his own, when Alice murmured, turning her face away:

'Is your daughter well?'

She must have known, since Gancel talked about him so often, that father and daughter had quarrelled, that they no longer saw each other, did not even greet one another when sometimes they met on one of the daughter's shopping trips to Le Havre.

She, in turn, had wanted to hurt him. He, for his part, could now comfortably hate this ugly and deformed girl who felt such adoration for her father but who must have hated the rest of the world and, that evening, him in particular.

'I assume my daughter is well. . . .'

And the mother said, to cover up what she thought had been a blunder:

'Do you think this dry weather will continue? It's been almost a month since it rained. . . .'

He thought of his daughter, of the car he had bought her, which she drove, often accompanied by her children, and which he passed in the streets and saw parked outside shops.

They never looked at each other. She probably did not even say to the children he had seen only as babies—and he had never seen the youngest:

'That man going by, with the bowler hat and the cigar, that's your grandfather.'

Or, more probably, she did. Knowing Berthe and her lack of feeling, he thought she might point him out as he went by:

'You see that ugly man? That's your grandfather. He's a bad man. He tried to ruin us for the sake of a woman.'

He looked at the three people. Why were they different from others? He could not believe that it was goodness that united them like that, because he did not believe in goodness. Man is not good.

The subject used to arise in the past with his sisters-in-law. They were always making claims of soft-heartedness and kindness.

'He's such a good man, Malétras. . . .'

And he would reply, chewing his cigar:

'If he's good at the moment, it's because he feels weak or unhappy. Man is only good when he needs other people.'

Nobody, except his mother, had ever been kind to him. He had never been kind, because he had never needed anybody.

He was convinced that it was not innate wickedness. He did not think himself crueller than the next man; it was just human pride.

When he was a small boy, he had always hidden to cry when he hurt himself, because he did not want anybody to console him, except possibly his mother.

They said:

'He's hard.'

Was it being hard to believe that man must fight alone, for himself, in life?

He had never borrowed one sou.

'There is no reason for anybody to give me money that I have not earned.'

Nor had he ever lent any. If anyone wanted his money, let them steal it at their own risk and peril, as he had done in the past from his bosses' till. If he had been caught, he would have taken his punishment without complaint.

'They are good,' he now told himself, 'because they need each other; they would be nothing without one another.'

And then a light seemed to come on in his mind. He ceased to be interested in his surroundings. They must have spoken to him but he did not hear what they said. He was far away. He was in Lulu's room.

He was on the point of understanding why he had chosen her, why, during those winter months, he had been impelled to go and see her every evening.

Was he not obscurely searching, without realising it, for someone who would owe him everything, someone who, like Madame Gancel, could not get up alone or perform the smallest human function without help, would not exist without him?

He rose.

'Are you going?'

'Yes. I've got another errand to do.'

A look from Madame Gancel to her daughter, a look that meant:

'Take him down.'

Alice obediently rose, but the father got up at the same time. 'I'll go.'

They went downstairs, one behind the other, and Malétras was gloomier as he left than when he had arrived. In the hall he said in a low voice:

'You know your son intended to kill himself?'

'He wouldn't have done it. He's young.'

'He had already chosen the place.'

The other man answered with a confidence designed to enrage Malétras further:

'He wrote to me about it.'

That was all. They shook hands. The street was dark now. There were stars in the sky, but no moon. Two shapes, far away, arm in arm, against the wall. The door closed. The chain inside was fixed; Gancel must be hastening back to join his family in the upstairs bedroom, whose light shone a bit more brightly from behind the curtains because of the darkness outside.

Malétras too wanted to huddle into his corner, and his corner was . . .

He walked fast, with his hands in his pockets. The streets were empty. He looked like a wealthy man. Perhaps one night someone would leap from the shadows and take from him, dead or alive, everything that he had on him. He was not afraid. He had never been afraid.

He crossed more brightly lit streets where people were enjoying the cool air at sidewalk cafés. He saw a man alone, a little apart from the others, at a table. An orchestra played inside the café. The sound of billiards could be heard through the open window on the floor above.

The man was middle-aged, a low-paid office worker, neatly dresssed, well brought up probably, with a timid expression; every time women went by, especially professionals, who looked him in the eyes, he jumped and turned away.

Who knows? Perhaps he was ashamed of his solitude, as if it were an embarrassing disease.

Dark streets again. Alleys. He rediscovered the smell, recognised fat Maria's door from far off, and went in and sat down, but felt immediately that there was something foreign and unfriendly here.

He had never come in the evening. He had never seen the little bistro with the lamp lit.

The curtain on the kitchen door moved. Maria was coming, but she only half opened the door, and shut it carefully behind her. She squeezed through the opening as if to prevent anyone seeing inside.

'I didn't recognise you right away. I wasn't expecting to see you at this time. What will you have?'

Why did she not bring him his anisette automatically, as she had on other occasions? She finally brought a glass, sat down for a minute beside him, and whispered:

'Could you wait a moment? I've got someone here. But I'll be with you soon. . . .'

She went to the threshold and leaned out, as if she was impatient or worried. She gave him an apologetic smile as she went by.

'Just coming! . . .' she promised in a low voice.

She went back into the kitchen, where he could see nothing, and for several minutes he heard two voices murmuring, hers and a man's.

At last there were hurried footsteps on the pavement. Somebody came in. He recognised her immediately.

It was the girl who had come once before when he had been there, the one about whom the proprietress had whispered to him:

'Would you like a little girl?'

She recognised him too. She was surprised. Smiling, she was about to go towards him, holding out her hand, when the kitchen door opened again:

'This way, Martine.'

'Oh! Yes.'

And her expression said:

'Good! I thought there must have been a mistake.'

The murmuring began again on the other side of the glass door and the lace curtain. Then there were footsteps on a staircase, which appeared to be inside the wall just behind Malétras's back. He heard somebody puffing on the way up.

'An old man,' he thought.

Somebody was walking above his head. They were moving furniture. A jug was put down somewhere.

At last old Maria came down again, leaving the kitchen door open this time, and sat down, apologising.

'It's a gentleman who's something important—I don't know what in, but I suspect it's the civil government. He comes on a regular day at this time. That slut Martine was late, like all these girls who know nothing about life. May I offer you a little drink for having kept you waiting? Yes, yes . . . You're not like the others, are you?'

There was a whole world of unexpressed thoughts in these last words. He was not a real customer. He did not come there 'for that.'

She dared not say that he was a friend. She was not yet completely sure about him.

'Don't worry. He won't come through here. When I hear that it's finished—and it never lasts long— I'll shut the kitchen door. He prefers not to see me afterwards. He's like that. You can hear him going into the yard on tiptoe and he leaves by the alley that comes out the other side of the cobbler's shop.'

She could not think of anything else to say. Despite the little drink she had given him, despite her confidential winks, despite the stories she told as to a regular or a friend, she felt that he was not happy and was thinking of going.

'It's a pity you came on his day! Other evenings, I'm mostly all alone . . .'

Did she realise that what she had said had great meaning for him?

All alone . . . So he came here, to this stinking street, in order to be alone with an old woman who dealt in little girls!

And Hermine despised him so much because she thought he was chasing little girls!

It was not that really. It was much more terrible. His flesh needed nothing. He was not depraved. He never had been. He felt nothing but disgust for the sounds that came through the thin ceiling.

'Other evenings,' old Maria had said, to restore his peace of mind, 'I'm mostly all alone.'

And indeed it was alone that he had hoped to find her, and he

82

had been vexed, jealous even—there was no other word for it—at the presence of another man behind the door.

Jealous of what?

He had a friend, Doctor Verel indeed, whom he saw every day at the Cintra, who had one day stormed out, furious, because their bridge table had been taken by some visiting English people whom the owners had not dared turn out.

He had sulked for a week. Every evening the others had to find a fourth, and they had been forced to go to his house, to argue with him and beg in order to bring him back to the Cintra.

Verel, who looked after the neurotic and the insane, jealous about a table and chair!

'Are you angry? I've got to live, haven't I? Oh, at my age you don't need much.'

He stared fixedly at her. She claimed that she had once been beautiful, and it was possible. Now her face was fat and moonlike and almost devoid of expression.

It was not age that made it like that. Perhaps she had always been as passive as her unobtrusive features indicated.

She had wandered all over the place, without fear, like a piece of paper blowing along the pavements. She had slept anywhere, with anybody, eaten and drunk anything, and was only now, at the end, afraid of one single thing, and that was a terminal illness in a hospital bed.

Lulu had not been afraid either. She had not worried about the present or the future. At first she tried to make Malétras believe that she had always been good, because she thought that would make him happy.

Then, faced with his insistence, thinking that, on the contrary, he would enjoy hearing her stories, she told him about her adventures as a waitress at the Frégate.

'He was a little redhead who didn't speak French.'

Or the man was like this or like that. . . .

And she had gone with them, for no reason, not because she enjoyed it—she admitted that she had always found it painful.

She had gone into unfamiliar rooms, undressed, gone to bed. . . .

'What about the diseased?' he would ask.

'If one had to think about that!'

'Suppose you had fallen in with a brute, or a maniac?'

She would shrug.

'Suppose you had had a child?'

Well, she would have had a child, that's all. She would have found someone to take care of it, or sent it to her mother.

When she had learned that he was rich, she was furious at having been duped—he had tricked her. At first she wanted to kick him out, and it only occurred to her afterwards to make something out of it.

What had she bought? A fur coat, in the middle of May!

And why had she taken Joseph as her lover? He was not handsome; he was unhealthy and unattractive, with his boils.

She was like that.

She had wanted to go for a drive at night in a big car. Perhaps Laniel had taken advantage of it to stop somewhere and enjoy her favours. If he had asked, she certainly would not have refused.

After all, one must pay one's way.

Too bad for her. Too bad for Malétras. She had wanted to dance and she had danced. If he had told her that if she danced, he would shoot her with a pistol, she would still have danced, just as she had refused to undress even when she had seen in his eyes that he was serious.

He took a mouthful of his nasty drink. He was ill at ease. Maria noticed it.

'It looks as though something's bothering you.'

Bothering, she called it! It was not just his present and future that were at stake, but his whole past, sixty years of life, sixty years of unceasing toil, which had left in all the innermost recesses of his being a feeling of crushing tiredness.

'Come on, have a little glass with Maria and you'll forget all about it.'

He smiled. That smile that had appeared for the first time, when he had felt so miserable, for the unknown Emile, who served him his port each evening. A smile of pity, more for himself than for others.

He did not like alcohol. He had never been a drinker. It was his third glass that evening. Maria's alcohol was strong and nasty, and yet he accepted it.

Then he saw her hurriedly shutting the kitchen door. A shadow passed behind it, fled through the yard; you could still hear the sound of water upstairs. Martine finally came down.

'Come and have a drink with us, my girl. You don't mind, do you?'

Martine must have wondered if it was she he was waiting for, and whether she was going to have to go up again. She sat down shyly on the chair she was offered, and smiled vaguely at him, with her hands on her fake crocodile bag, her stockings rolled down below knees, which stuck out from her acid-green dress.

She was probably not thinking about anything.

8

It was in the street, later, a street he did not know and never found again—although there was a curious house, reached not by going up, but by going down five or six steps, which he nearly fell down, as if through a trap door—it was in this street, at about eleven o'clock, or midnight at the latest, that he made his decision.

He was to remember that precisely, and the house with the steps that led down from the street. He was lucid. He could see himself wandering the streets like a sick dog.

Had he been drunk earlier? It was hard to say. He had been drunk only once in his life, on the night before he was conscripted. They had all landed in the dance hall of a café where there was no music that day. It was a foretaste of the barracks, with its vast expanse of grey floor, ugly green walls, and backless benches.

He was with boys from his district, who had hitherto respected him because he was more educated and had kept them at a distance.

But that evening, perhaps because they had seen him naked like the others, they treated him as an equal, and he soon became their scapegoat. He had been drinking without being aware of it. He became angry at every burst of laughter, and the angrier he became the more excited they got. Finally, he had collapsed in the midst of them, absurd and pitiful, and had been disgustingly sick.

He had never been drunk since, except possibly this evening.

He had not been aware of drinking. He had been to Gancel's house, where they had given him one single small glass. Then, at Maria's, two glasses before Martine came down. He had bought a round. Had Maria then bought another? Probably. He had not noticed.

He did not feel drunk at that moment—merely in an extraordinary state, a state of heightened sensibility. Things that he had until then only vaguely guessed at seemed to acquire an amazing clarity.

Hermine, for example. He could now see her from a great height. How small she seemed, how petty and ridiculous, with her pathetic self-assurance and her superior smile!

He had made a mistake in choosing a wife who did not need him; that was all. She had a small personal fortune. She talked about it enough, poor thing: not boastfully, but, on the contrary, with discreet allusions, but these allusions were just as ridiculous as the boasts of a *nouveau riche* like himself.

When she sat down in front of her little desk in the evening, with her glasses on her nose, and a look of slightly solemn satisfaction, it was apparent that she was about to write to one of her farmers or tenants about roof repairs or a mortgage.

Her way of saying 'my lawyer . . .'

Or ' my uncle Kenavan . . .' or 'my aunt de la Lourcerie . . .'

She received little bequests from here and there, because nobody in her family was poor, or if they were, she did not mention them; all had a little property, all had lawyers. She would speak with extra enthusiasm about a particular cousin who owned a racing stable in Paris, and from whom she expected to inherit, as did about forty others.

She was very proud of being 'well-born' , as she called it, though only once, it was true. Proud of having been a general's wife. As for his money, it was vulgar, common money.

There . . .

He had thought of all this at Maria's, sitting between the two women, while Martine looked at him curiously, perhaps still wondering the same thing.

Was it obvious that he had been drinking? Probably, because Maria too looked at him oddly. He thought that he could see, as if through a fog, pity in her eyes, and that annoyed him. He did not want anyone's pity. He would not allow pity.

At Gancel's house they had not felt pity for him. They had not suspected why he had come. They had been mistaken about his visit, particularly the daughter, that nightmare creature whose pale face haunted him. She had thought it was out of gratuitous wickedness.

Why was Maria sorry for him? Was it because she was beginning to suspect the truth, to guess why he came to see her?

He had no vices, no murky desires. He came . . . how could

he put it? Because he had no place anywhere else. That was not quite true. He came because it was like a last refuge.

No! He could not make his thoughts more precise. Anyway, it was disagreeable and humiliating.

It was an evening of humiliations. He had been humiliated leaving his house, humiliated going to Gancel's, humiliated . . . To think that they were there, all three of them, in that huge room pervaded by sickness and death, talking about him, and possibly pitying him!

This was, more or less, what he had thought and felt. Suddenly he stood up, and then, to show these two women they were wrong about him, to make them believe that he was a man like all the rest and did not need their pity, he turned towards the kitchen door and looked at the ceiling for a moment, which they immediately understood.

'You want to?' Maria said astonished, calling him 'tu' for the first time, just when their relationship was becoming, as it were, a professional one. Martine!

'Yes.'

Martine went ahead of him. He stumbled on the narrow staircase, already regretting his stupid decision, but it was too late, the lights were being turned on. There was a red silk handkerchief with a wooden acorn at each corner over the lamp-shade.

Maria remade the bed. The rug on the floor was so worn that its original colour could no longer be guessed. You could see only the thread. Martine poured some water into a basin.

'It's for you,' she said. 'I washed before coming down.'

In other words, after the other one, the man who was probably something in the civil government.

It was funny. He must have been drunk because he felt himself swaying slightly as he stood in the middle of the room. But he noticed Maria showing some final hesitation, as though she had some compunction about leaving them alone. What was she afraid of?

At last! She went heavily down the stairs, whilst Martine pulled her dress over her head, pushed the straps of her slip over her thin shoulders and let it fall to the floor. She was wearing nothing but her stockings, rolled down below her knees.

She asked:

'Shall I take them off?'

Did he answer? He no longer had any idea. He had felt a slight pinching in his chest and he stood still, frightened, wondering

87

what was happening to his body. He had always imagined that one day he could collapse just like that, and he thought now about a politician, much talked about a few years earlier, who had died in a similar place.

'Aren't you coming?'

She was lying across the bed looking at the ceiling: her legs hung down; like a young man, he turned his eyes away from the obscene ink-black triangle.

He should have left then. Or, no. If he had gone then, he would not have felt himself touching rock bottom; he would have hung on to something or other.

He remembered now a thick silence, his own noisy breathing, the girl's face turning towards him, surprised, slightly pitying, but also slightly irritated.

Quite a long time had passed when he heard Maria, who was listening at the door, thinking she was not making any noise.

It was atrocious, revolting. He wanted to get up, but it was Martine who persisted. Goodness knows why, perhaps out of some kind of vanity, or perhaps she was afraid of the old lady's reproaches.

When he finally went down, with his waistcoat buttoned wrong, he must have looked frightful. He had such a hard look that Maria asked:

'Aren't you happy? Wasn't she nice?'

He nearly went out without answering, without paying, wanting to push aside everything that blocked his way. Only on the threshold did he remember the last act he had to perform. He took out his wallet and offered two or three notes, without counting them. He did not say good-bye. He did not turn round.

It was over. He had walked for a long time, dragging himself through the streets like a sick animal—that was it, a sick animal. The difference being, however, that he felt his chest from time to time, and was afraid, breaking out in a cold sweat at the thought of a possible accident.

He would be ill. That was settled. All his life he had cherished that thought, and it was as comforting as a dream. When he felt himself teetering on the brink of the void, he told himself that one day he would go to bed; he would be ill, and then he would see only kind faces around him.

He would no longer have to think or make decisions. They would think and work things out for him.

All would be sweetness. . . . Sweetness! A word he did not know the meaning of, something he had never tasted.

People around a sick person try to smile and create a reassuring world, like the world of children's pictures.

He was ill, he was going to be ill. It was the only escape. Perhaps his illness would be real. He knew that he would only have to lie down to make it real.

At one point, at a street corner where he could see two policemen in capes leaning on their bicycles, he wondered whether he might not become ill there and then.

He would only have to let himself slide to the ground. They would rush to him. No doubt someone would ring for an ambulance. They would take him to a hospital. . . . No, he would still have the strength to tell them who he was, to demand the comfort of a private clinic.

'One of our most distinguished citizens,' it would say the next day in the local papers, 'was taken ill whilst . . .'

No! It would be better to be ill at home, to force Hermine to take care of him, to be gentle and indulgent. Perhaps they would summon his daughter?

His head was spinning, his chest was gripped by fear, and he began to walk faster, leaning forward slightly.

His key was in his pocket. He could have taken it out and gone in without disturbing anyone. He rang.

Perhaps they were all asleep already? He did not know what time it was. After a few moments the light came on in the hall and the door opened. Rose was standing before him, dressed in her everyday clothes, probably wondering why he did not come in, why he stood in the doorway looking at her.

Then he saw that he had frightened her. She was about to run away, screaming.

He opened his mouth and breathed:

'It's I, Rose. . . . Is madame here?'

Was he really ill, iller than he thought? He moved forward. There were five marble steps to climb. It reminded him of the steps of the sunken house. God, what street was that? It must have been a long way away. He must have walked a lot, for hours.

'Is something wrong, monsieur?'

He had stopped on the second step, aware that his heart was also about to stop. Rose rushed past him to the bottom of the inside stairs, shouting:

89

'Madame! ... Madame! ... Come down quickly! ...
Monsieur is ...'

He smiled. It was his last clear image: he was on the second step, standing, one hand on his chest, smiling vaguely; he could see Rose's black dress, her embroidered apron, her white cap. He thought ...

He did not fall all at once. He had the presence of mind to go down the two steps, lean forward, crouch, and let himself sink gently to the stone staircase.

Now the maid could scream and rush about the house like a madwoman.

Malétras, no doubt because the marble was cold, began to shake convulsively.

9

It began with a fly. His eyes were closed. His body was immobile, inert; no doubt he was still partly asleep; in any case, he seemed to be incapable of moving. The fly buzzed around him; he followed it, waited for it. His alerted senses tried to predict where it might land—his nose, his forehead, his head, the sweat-soaked pillow?

It was more than fifty years since Malétras had bothered about flies, since they had ever existed for him. He knew they existed—people hung flypaper in their rooms, and he had sold it wholesale. Perhaps without realising it, he had brushed aside flies which buzzed around him as he read his newspaper.

For more than fifty years he had not been conscious of the life of flies. Now, after so long, he recognised this one, although he could not see because his eyes were shut. It was a fly he associated with staying in bed late. Since, even as a child, Malétras had never stayed in bed unless forced to, it was a fly belonging to a morning of illness. A morning when he had mumps, an illness that had kept him in bed for three days.

It was a May or June fly, when the summer is not yet too hot and one has not yet become used to it.

The sun did not flood into the room—he did not need to open his eyes to see that—it peeked through the slits in the blind, and the wall and bed, and Malétras himself, were striped with shade and golden light.

The fly landed on his forehead. The tickling was similar to that of the past, both maddening and exciting. Malétras prevented himself from pulling his hand out from under the sheet. He felt that he could not resist much longer and just when he could not stand it any more, the fly took off, turned, described large and small circles, went away, came back, and he wondered again where he would feel the little dancing feet. . . .

Oh! He did not delude himself! He had no fever.

He was clearheaded, dreadfully clearheaded, although hardly awake. He knew that what lay there was Jules Malétras's old carcass, a large worn-out body and a face covered with grey hairs as hard as bristle. The fly must have seen him as even more monstrous than he was, terrifying—perhaps that was why it buzzed round and round for so long before settling, and then only remained in one place for a moment.

Something rose in his throat like a bubble of air. An unformed thought, a vague longing, floated from his mind, detached itself from him and immediately vanished, leaving a slight dampness beneath his thick, smarting eyelids. For a second, a tenth of a second, he wanted . . . No, it was not as precise as that. . . . How could he put it? . . . To be still the young boy with mumps, with taut pink skin! To escape from this disgusting carcass, to have done with this worn, thickened skin, the rough hairs, the hoarse breathing . . .

All this translated itself into an image, and then into smells, those of Saturday evening in the kitchen behind the shop, being washed in the tub full of soapy water.

Afterwards he smelled clean and fresh, even outside on Place de l'Eglise.

Why was it not possible once you were a man, once you were old, to be thoroughly clean, both body and soul?

He was not sad. He did not rebel. He would never rebel again. He felt that he knew everything. For example, he felt that he could draw up a meticulous balance sheet of the night he had just lived through, not with words and sentences, but, he thought, with numbers, precise numbers, written with a steel nib in very black ink on the hard paper of one of the big Malétras account books.

He needed only to half open his eyelids to know what time it was. He heard, on the white marble mantelpiece, the ticking of the gilded bronze Louis XVI clock that came, as they said in the house, from Hermine's side. But he did not need the help of the hands and the elegant numerals on the bulging clock face.The fly, the smell of the house, the noises in the street placed this moment in the middle of the morning, between ten and half past.

Somebody he had never seen before was going to and fro near him. He could hear a particular rustle, not of a soft dress, but of a starched apron, a nurse's apron. Sometimes the person came and looked at him; he remained quiet, like a man asleep. Once, his wrist was gently picked up. He knew that she was taking his pulse and he nearly smiled; he had to make an effort to keep his lips still.

He had known beforehand that there would be a nurse by him when he woke. He also knew that he was no longer ill. The torpor that remained in his limbs was caused by the same thing as had caused the insipid, not unpleasant aftertaste in his mouth: it was the medicine he had been given three times in three hours.

The attack had lasted for three hours. During that time his eyes had been open, and he had followed, every quarter of an hour, the progress of the gilt hands on the Louis XVI clock face.

He had not lost consciousness for a moment. He had probably never been so lucid in his life.

Downstairs in the white-flagged hall, he had thought he was going to faint. The world had spun around him, but the unconsciousness he hoped for, yearned for, as a release, did not come.

He remained collapsed and limp at the bottom of the steps while Rose rushed screaming up to the next floor. He was so conscious that he thought:

'The two of them will never be able to carry me. They'll have to wake up Eugénie.'

Then, immediately:

'My breath must smell of alcohol, and Hermine will think I am drunk.'

He thought that and he was convinced that he was going to die. His main wish was to reach his bed, and he was terrified by the insurmountable obstacles that separated him from it.

Hermine came down, frightened by the maid's cries, wearing her blue print dressing gown with a big lace collar. He preferred to keep his eyes shut.

She felt him. She was about to panic. She spoke to him.

'Can you hear me?'

They both circled round his huge mass, took him under the

arms, managed to make him sit up, and he knew he would have to help them. Supported by the two women, he made an effort and stood up.

On the stairs, so as not to waste any time, Hermine shouted to the cook, who slept on the second floor:

'Eugénie! Eugénie! . . . Monsieur is ill. . . . Come down quickly. . . . Eugénie!. . .'

He remembered her saying furiously when Eugénie did not hear:

'That old cat is deaf!'

He had been pushed, dragged, heaved like a dead body, and finally dropped onto the edge of his bed, where he sat with his arms dangling, his eyes wandering.

He was going to die. He was convinced of that. Some mechanism inside him was about to stop at any second. They were questioning him. How absurd to question him—he was incapable of answering; he needed all his strength for himself, to focus entirely on his inner self.

Why could he still hear and understand? Rose running up the stairs, banging on a door like a madwoman, footsteps above his head, fat, moon-faced Eugénie getting up.

'Rose. . . . Well, Rose?' Hermine was losing patience. 'Telephone Doctor Verel, quickly. . . . His number is written above the telephone. Tell him to come at once. . . . Tell him that monsieur . . .'

No doubt she had, like everybody else, thought about death from time to time, but never as she did that night.

It was stupid!

There was no other word for it. It was tragically stupid! Rose telephoning; Eugénie being told to light the fire, goodness knows why; Hermine watching him, telling him to lie down, becoming impatient, almost angry with him because he persisted in remaining on the edge of the bed, with his body leaning forward, both hands on his chest.

He could not explain to her that if he lay down, it would all be over. It felt as if the slightest movement might stop the invisible machine, which was still working inside him but which might break down at any moment.

She was not crying. She must have been thinking about death too, though not in the same way. He now understood deathbed dramas. Everybody thinks about death. But only one person thinks about it for himself. The others know that in the morning the sun will come through the blinds and their coffee will be served.

His shoes were dirty. He could see them and the mud on his trousers. Could that really affect him?

'Well! . . . Verel? . . .' he managed to articulate when everything began to dissolve around him.

'He's coming. . . . Keep calm. . . . Rose has telephoned him. He's coming at once. . . .'

What strange curiosity there was in Hermine's eyes! Respectful curiosity. Because he was probably going to die.

'Rose! Go downstairs and stay by the door so that you can let Doctor Verel in as soon as you hear his car.'

God, it was stupid! He had hardly had time to live! He had hardly noticed himself living! He had always worked, only worked. What untiring efforts, what a huge amount of toil and willpower—he felt it like a crushing weight on his shoulders.

And then, suddenly, just like that . . .

He rose. Hermine was frightened and wanted to force him to sit down. He resisted. She did not understand that by standing up he was a little further from death. They must be quick. Verel must arrive. The time had come. He could no longer defend himself alone.

At last—voices on the stairs. Hermine rushed out, whispered on the landing, and that fool felt obliged to go through his little act.

'Now, old fellow, not feeling too well? Let's see your eyes. . . . So . . . It doesn't seem too serious. . . .'

He had brought his bag. He looked around automatically for somewhere to wash his hands, and rolled up his sleeves.

'Help me to undress him.'

Now Malétras was shaking. He was cold. Perhaps it was fear. His pale, furry chest was laid bare. A towel was placed on it. Hermine leaned forward to see the doctor's face.

'Tell my chauffeur to come up. . . . You wouldn't like to lie down, would you, Malétras?. . . Put a dressing gown on him.'

'He's shaking.'

'Have you got any ice?'

'There's some downstairs.'

Rose, who had been on the landing, near the open door, had fetched the chauffeur, who now stood, cap in hand, shifting from one foot to the other.

They were talking in low voices. Malétras could hear.

'Listen, Désiré, go to Professor Picard's. . . . You know where he lives?'

'Yes, sir.'

'Bring him back. . . . Tell him . . .'

He mumbled the rest, but Malétras guessed. It was serious. It was urgent.

Eugénie was on the stairs. She was sent to get some ice.

As for Hermine, she tried to draw Verel to the landing to question him, but he pretended not to understand.

'Don't worry, Malétras. . . . It'll pass. . . . Since it's not in my department, I've sent for Professor Picard. You must know Picard? . . . Of course you do!'

He talked and talked. He was not threatened by sudden death. From time to time, he would glance at Malétras's face with a sharp, brief look. Perhaps he was a bit sorry for him. The next day, at five o'clock at the Cintra, he would announce:

'By the way, poor old Malétras won't be coming any more. I was called to his house last night, and . . .'

From time to time Malétras managed to give a light sigh, which relieved him, and then he would risk raising his head and looking around him.

The others were part of the living; that was why they were embarrassed by his stare, tried to smile, immediately felt they had to say almost anything.

How stupid it was!

Ten to one already. The white marble fireplace . . . It was Hermine who had wanted a white marble fireplace. . . . When he had seen it for the first time, Malétras had been pleased, because it gave the room a particularly luxurious effect that was new to him.

'Here's the ice, madame. Where shall I put it?'

Eugénie had brought the ice tray from the refrigerator, with its regular squares of ice, like the ones they put in orangeade when visitors came.

'Have you got a rubber hot-water bottle, and a glass?'

The pain was returning in strength. He could feel it coming. It grew and grew. He felt as if it were lifting him, his feet no longer touching the ground; everything was going to disappear. He opened his mouth to cry out in fear, or, rather, he wanted to open his mouth, but he did not dare, he did not want to lose any energy. Like a rocket reaching its climax, it burst through his body and crumbled into a thousand smaller stabs, which dissolved little by little and left him a moment of respite.

Professor Picard, whom Malétras until then had only glimpsed, an elegant, very wealthy man with rather abrupt manners, came into the room and shook Verel's hand.

He said nothing, and got his instruments out of his bag.

'What time did the attack begin?'

He had turned towards Verel, but it was Hermine who replied.

'He came in a little after midnight. He fell suddenly in the hall downstairs. . . .'

Malétras no longer counted. He was there only as an object to be examined, talked about in low, and sometimes loud, voices.

'Don't you think, Professor, that he would be better off in his bed? He's shivering.'

No reply.

'Could you give me half a glass of water?'

He took a thin packet of powder out of his pocket and dissolved it with the end of his gold pen.

'Drink it. . . . Drink it slowly. . . . It's not bad.'

Not bad! What could it matter whether it tasted bad or not?

'I thought an application of ice on the heart . . .' Verel said.

He was approved with a movement of the head.

After that, all they could do was wait. They waited, the two doctors and Hermine in the bedroom, Rose on the landing, Eugénie and Verel's chauffeur in the kitchen, where Eugénie was making coffee just in case.

They waited in silence at first. Then, as if by chance, the doctors found themselves together near the farthest window, and talked in low voices. Hermine was probably dying to join them, but she dared not go over immediately. She asked, without thinking what she was saying:

'Are you feeling better?'

And Malétras knew perfectly well that she was going to go towards the window; he could predict the questions, and could even predict the professor's shrug, which seemed to say:

'One can't tell yet. . . .'

His senses were so acute that he overheard the word 'daughter' even though it was mumbled.

'Do you think I should call his daughter?'

What could the professor say? That man did not know. He was not inside Malétras's skin.

The only thing he had been able to do for him was give him some medicine. They would see what effect that would have.

Malétras was alone. True, he had often been conscious of his own solitude. This time it was different. He realised how totally alone he was, he realised once and for all that man, whatever he does, is alone in life and in death.

Hermine was thinking of bringing his daughter to his bedside. She was ready to send telegrams, make telephone calls. Who knows? She was perhaps partly reacting to her need to leave this room for a while, escape from this maddening wait, and not be there at the most disagreeable moment.

Twice she came back towards her husband. Twice she returned to the doctors. Finally she left the room, went down to the study; he heard her telephoning.

If his daughter came, if she was present, what difference would it make? If anyone was there . . .

One-thirty-five. The professor half filled the glass of water and emptied another packet of powder into it.

'Drink. . . . I think it's beginning to work. . . . You're feeling a bit better, aren't you?'

He shook his head and realised that it was a matter of complete indifference to the professor, who was suffering from not being able to light a cigarette. Twice he had pulled a very fine case out of his pocket. When it was over and he was back in his car, he could at last . . .

Malétras, meanwhile, was searching for something to hang on to, a picture, a memory: when his son was born, for example, and . . . No! His son was dead. All he could see of him was that odious notebook. His wife . . . his daughter . . .

He could find nothing, just emptiness and turmoil; he felt he had reached a void, and he would have to go further back in time, search through his early childhood memories.

But then, if his childhood was the only thing that mattered, what was the use?

Hermine came back up, embarrassed, and tried to smile at him. 'Are you feeling better?'

She was begging, and he avoided saying no. He did not know any more. He was a battlefield. Opposing forces were struggling inside him, and he was not capable of helping one of them; he could only retreat into himself and listen to the echoes of the battle, the beating of the invisible machine.

Why was Rose sniffing on the stairs? She did not like Malétras.

She had no reason to like him. It was the atmosphere of the house that was affecting her.

The doorbell rang. Who had been summoned? It could not be his daughter—she did not live in Le Havre. Hermine rushed down, and he had a flash of intuition: she had gone off guiltily, with a nervous look. She had called a priest!

The proof that it was a priest was that the visitor did not come up, but was shown into the study, and that Hermine remained with him for a good while. When she came back, she went and spoke quietly to the two doctors, who did not know what to say to her.

At ten past two he sat on the edge of the bed, and they gave him his third dose of medicine. The lulls were longer and more frequent. Despite the ice, which he was holding against his chest, and which had already been renewed, he no longer felt cold.

He was floating. He was a long way above them all, above all men.

'Doctor, don't you think that he's already a better colour?'

Yes! He did not need the mirror. He could feel the blood beginning to circulate again in his arteries. But he could not yet submit to lying down. He was still racked by fear.

Sometimes he heard a boat's siren, sometimes a train. It was a good sign, because for two hours, until the priest rang the doorbell, he had heard nothing of life outside his room.

Eugénie had brought up coffee and cups on a tray. Didn't people eat at funerals too? Hermine suggested:

'Won't you have a little drink?'

The two doctors refused, but had they not been in front of Malétras . . .

Well, now . . . he was not dead. He was not going to die; he was almost sure of that. A voluptuous heat spread through him, more inside than out. Something flowed through his limbs. He did not want them to see this yet. He wanted to be sure. He stared at the white face of the clock. He felt that he was following the imperceptible movement of the hands.

And at last, at exactly ten past three, he could not help heaving a deep sigh. The rocket had gone up very high, much higher than all the others. It had turned into a huge spray, which had spread to the extremities of his body. He had felt inflated to the point of leaving the ground, and in less than a second all the pain had left his body.

He was once again a man like any other.

He was not dead. He had no more reason to be dead than the next person. The proof was that he was standing up by himself. Hermine cried out, thinking that perhaps he was delirious:

'What are you doing?'

He was going to pee! That was the reaction. He was capable of going to pee alone in his own bathroom.

He was floating slightly. His movements were hazy. Hermine wanted to help him, but he pushed her away, and it was Verel who accompanied him into the bathroom.

'You're saved, old fellow. . . . You gave us a fright, but it's over now. . . . Picard was saying that a few minutes ago. As long as he can get through the attack . . . A good night's sleep and you won't know anything happened. . . .'

Why did Malétras give a fiercely sarcastic smile?

'I think Picard will give you an injection, so that you sleep for about ten hours. . . .'

It was all the same to him.

'What about the priest?' he said in a loud sarcastic voice that his wife must have heard.

'Madame Malétras thought she was doing the best thing. . . . Would you like me to help you undress?'

He was still wearing his filthy trousers and shoes.

When he went back into the room, his wife, helped by Rose, was busy remaking the big bed. She had turned on the night light on the table, and all disorder had vanished.

'How are you feeling? Lie down now. . . . The professor will give you an injection so that you can get some rest.'

What made them all so awkward? Was it the expression on his face? He felt that he did not have his usual expression. He was not, properly speaking, smiling, but his features had lost their hardness. He was relaxed, was still floating a little. He looked at everything around him with extraordinary detachment, mingled with irony and perhaps a little scorn.

He was being as docile as a child. He seemed to be saying:

'Now do with me what you wish. It's all the same to me. I've nothing more in common with you.'

He heard them mention a nurse. Hermine, out of regard for principle and tradition, because she wanted to be the devoted wife to the end, the wife who does her duty, and more, said that she would be capable of sitting with him and looking after him.

Then Malétras turned towards Verel as if towards a fellow

conspirator, and said simply, in a way that allowed no disagreement:

'A nurse!'

He lay down. They bared his thigh for an injection. Rose turned her head away.

There was a little more agitation around him, some whispering, things moved around. The front door opened and closed again; a car drove off in the night, almost the dawn now.

Later he knew they were putting up a bed for Hermine in the bathroom, and then, finally, he went to sleep.

He knew everything. The nurse, while he had been asleep, had arranged the room as she wanted it. Hermine must have gone to sleep in the spare room at the end of the hall, so that the nurse could have her place in the bathroom.

The household was awake. He discerned familiar sounds. In his sleep he seemed to have heard the sound of letters falling into the bottom of the letter box, and the postman's footsteps going away.

He was playing the fly game. He felt it about to land on him and he experienced a delicious shiver as he waited, impatient, for the moment when the tickling on his forehead began.

He would like to have gone on for a long time, but he felt a throbbing urge, as he had when he was a child with mumps and would hold on until the last moment and then jump onto the rug and seize his chamber pot.

He could hold on no longer. He opened his eyes, and saw beside his bed a table he did not recognise, which must have been brought down from the attic and was covered with a white cloth. On it were carefully arranged bottles and glasses.

His first thought was to get up, and he threw back the cover, but at that moment the nurse approached, with no other sound than the dry, almost brittle rustle of her starched apron.

'Did you sleep well?'

He was disappointed. She was neither beautiful nor pretty. She must have been forty. She was short, solid, with hard features and the calm, orderly look of a woman doing her duty.

'Do you need something?'

'I want . . .' he began, and turned towards the bathroom.

'Don't move. . . . You mustn't get up today. The professor has prescribed complete rest.'

She understood perfectly and slid beneath him, with a

conjuror's movement, almost without touching him, a porcelain bowl of a shape he had seen only during his first wife's illness.

'Stay calm. . . . In half an hour . . . At eleven o'clock the professor will come and see you.'

He had never been modest, never had any of that kind of refinement, but now he found it the most difficult thing in the world to urinate in her presence. She could not see anything, but the thought that she would hear . . .

She must have understood. She was used to ill men. She went over to raise the blinds, letting the sun flood into the room. When she came back, she withdrew the basin with the same ease, as if she were juggling, removed it from the room, then took a thermometer from a glass and shook it before slipping it between his lips.

'Shut your mouth. Don't move. Madame asked me to wake her up as soon as . . .'

She was going towards the door. He stopped her by vigorously shaking his head. Let Hermine go on sleeping. He did not need her. He had no wish to see her.

'She'll scold me.'

He shrugged, with the thermometer in his mouth, and he must have appeared comic like that because the nurse turned away to smile.

The room had never been so bright and orderly, and, curiously, the table with the bottles, instead of giving the room a gloomy or ambiguous purpose, made it seem reassuring, almost cheerful.

The thermometer was removed from his mouth as if he were a child.

'You haven't the slightest temperature. On the contrary!'

'How much?' he asked, for the sake of saying something, because he did not really care.

'Normal, 36.7 . . .'

He must have made her smile again when he said, with unexpected conviction:

'I'm hungry.'

'I can't give you anything before the professor comes. He will decide whether you can eat or not.'

'All right.'

He said 'All right' in a sulky tone, not recognising his own voice. For a few more minutes he gazed at the ceiling, where a small circle of sunlight flickered. Then he looked around for his fly, but turning his head in every direction tired him and he shut his eyes and waited for the professor to arrive.

10

The paper was bluish, the ink blue, the writing long, with remarkably regular downstrokes.

> Madame,
> I think it is my duty to let you know that during the night of the 26th your father suffered a rather serious attack of angina pectoris. I immediately summoned Professor Picard, who continues to attend him. According to him, although the patient's condition is satisfactory, a relapse is always a possibility.
>
> Yours sincerely,
Hermine Malétras

In an earlier version, now torn up and in the wastepaper basket, she had added:

'I would see no inconvenience in your coming to visit him.'

Hermine was in the right. The quarrel had not been of her making. Besides, she had nothing to expect from Berthe Laniel. She was the one who had been seized with a sudden hatred for Hermine—they had been friends before that—when the question of marriage had arisen. It was Berthe too who had been the first to stop greeting her.

Should she, because of that, prevent her from coming to her father's bedside? On the contrary, Hermine had at first wanted to make this return easy for her.

'I would see no inconvenience in your coming to visit him.'

Just the same, sitting at the little desk in the boudoir, she had stiffened a little as she reread these words. After all, she was a de Dodeville. She had her own fortune. By writing like that, did she not appear to be taking the first step, apologising almost?

'She'll come rushing, with or without that sentence.'

She stamped the letter and sent it express. A telegram would have been appropriate the night before, but not now that the danger seemed to have passed.

Hermine came and went in the huge house, always calm and diligent, with an eye on everything, foreseeing that her husband's illness would mean visitors.

Berthe Laniel received the letter towards the end of the afternoon in her villa near Caen. Her husband was at the garage. She telephoned to tell him to come home at once, then, with the receiver in her hand, she changed her mind—this unexpected news made her restless and she preferred to go herself.

'Wait for me. I'll come and see you.'

The children were with their governess, and she kissed them before going out with the car.

'My father nearly died last night,' she said to her husband, once they were in the little glassed-in office he kept for himself at the back of the garage.

He did not dare tell her that he had recently seen Malétras in good health, that he had even lent him a small sum of money.

'What was it?'

'An attack of angina pectoris. At least that's what she said. What are we going to do? Suppose you telephone Picard, who's looking after him, to see if there really is any danger?'

'Get me Doctor Picard's number in Le Havre, Mademoiselle Jenny.'

The secretary, in another glassed-in office, could be seen leafing through the directory.

'Hello? Is Doctor Picard there? In consultation? It's urgent, yes. Ten minutes, you say. All right, I'll ring back.'

They waited, buried in their separate thoughts, vaguely watching the comings and goings in the garage.

'Perhaps we should speak to the lawyer before anything else,' Berthe murmured just as her husband was picking up the receiver again.

'Hello! . . . Professor Picard? . . . This is Etienne Laniel, Monsieur Malétras's son-in-law. I've just heard the news. . . . Yes . . . My wife is very worried and would like to know . . . What?. . . Yes . . . Yes . . . I understand. . . . Of course . . . Yes. . . .'

Berthe picked up a second phone to listen, but it was too late, the conversation was coming to an end.

'Thank you, doctor. Please forgive me for having disturbed you. . . .'

And, to his wife:

'It appears that the attack was very violent and, for three hours he was inches away from death. At the moment one can't really say anything. The chances are he couldn't withstand another attack, but that might happen just as easily in the next hour or the next three years.'

'What should I do?'

'Decide.'

'Perhaps it would be better if you went to see him first?'

In the huge garage, seven or eight mechanics were busy repairing cars. The uniformed pump attendant stood by the metal door.

They talked for a good while, both calm.

'If we went this evening, it would look as if we were in too much of a hurry.'

'Tomorrow morning.'

'I have to go to Le Havre anyway for a fitting.'

'Let's go together.'

So it was decided: they would go together. Laniel would call on his father-in-law, and when he met his wife afterwards, they could decide how Berthe should behave.

It was one more worry, that was all.

At the Cintra, during the game, Doctor Verel announced, as if he had suddenly remembered it:

'By the way, poor old Malétras nearly had it last night.'

Steuvels looked at him with that anxiety he felt every time a man of his age died or was in danger of dying. Devismes went on dealing the cards. Legrand-Beaujon said, turning towards Malétras's empty place:

'That must be why we haven't seen him today.'

'What's the matter with him?'

'Angina pectoris.'

'Will he pull through?'

'For a time. I don't know how long. It all depends. Anyway, he had a real scare. We were by his bed for three hours with Picard, wondering if he was going to die on us.'

The three hours were going to become a byword. They would repeat:

'I've a friend, Malétras, the one from the Docks, who spent three hours between life and death.'

Devismes suggested:

'Perhaps one of us ought to go and see him?'

It was through Devismes, with whom he was in business, that Gancel heard about Malétras's illness. He wondered if he should mention it at home; he avoided as much as possible mentioning anything that might lower his wife's spirits.

'It's curious,' he murmured, however, after dinner. 'I was wondering why Malétras came to see us. Now I hear that he had a bad attack of angina that same night. I wonder now whether he had a foreboding.'

'Why would he come to see us if he felt ill?' asked his wife.

Alice, their daughter, cut in sourly:

'Perhaps because he couldn't find anyone else to feel sorry for him!'

'I shall go and see him tomorrow. If I know him, it must have been worse for him than for anyone else.'

Malétras was in his bed, and his world was limited by the four pale walls of his bedroom, in which the nurse came and went soundlessly. He did not complain, and remained quiet most of the time, gazing at some point in the room, the clock, for example, or the reflection on a bottle, or the pink satin bedcover. Or else he would close his eyes without actually sleeping.

'Do you need anything?'

'No, thank you.'

He was very polite to the nurse, whose name was Madame Hamom, showing unhoped-for docility. He had insisted on only one thing, which he cared about very much, a visit from the barber, who had shaved him by midday.

He had asked for a mirror, and stared at himself for a long time. When Madame Hamon wanted to put the mirror back, he had said to her with a touch of irritabilty:

'Leave that.'

He obeyed Professor Picard's instructions to the letter, but without attaching the niggling importance to them that some patients did.

The professor had been quite surprised when he came to see him in the morning. He was expecting the usual terrified questions. But Malétras had let himself be examined without a word. It was almost as though he were not the one concerned. When he looked at the professor, it was not to catch his reactions. It was an indifferent look. Perhaps he was looking at him without seeing him?

'A few more days of complete rest and you'll be on your feet. I would just advise you, even then, to avoid fatigue and excitement. Provided you take these precautions, you could live another twenty years.'

His eyes betrayed no happiness. Did he believe it? Did he disbelieve it? Was it all the same to him whether he died or not?

Hermine showed the professor down to the ground floor and into the boudoir.

'What do you think, doctor?'

'I think he's as well as can be expected.'

'I'm not talking about his heart.'

He waited, like a man who does not understand.

'I've been married to him for more than six years. I must know him, mustn't I? Well, doctor, he frightens me. I think something in him has changed.'

'What do you find abnormal about him?'

'He's not the same man. I don't know how to explain myself. When he looks at me, his stare embarrasses me so that I'm quite upset.'

'Perhaps it's still the effect of the injection?'

'I don't think so. Anyway, it doesn't exactly date from today. For some time I have felt a detachment that isn't in character.'

'If I understand you, you think he's in the grip of some new preoccupation?'

'Yes, doctor . . . No . . . It's not quite that either. . . .'

She sensed the shades of meaning. To express what she was really thinking, she could only have used words that were much too precise and that modesty prevented her from saying.

'This morning I wondered whether he recognised me.'

He looked at her in such a way that she blushed.

'I understand. But this is no longer my department. Since Doctor Verel is a friend of yours, you should speak with him.'

'I'm so sorry, doctor. . . .'

She could not get rid of the idea. She went up to his bedroom ten times. Obviously, Malétras recognised her footstep, her cautious way of opening the door noiselessly and without causing a draft. But he never gave the slightest sign that he knew she was nearby. He kept his eyes shut, or continued staring at a point in space.

She approached on tiptoe, leaned down, and murmured:

'Are you feeling all right?'

Then, reluctantly, like a man being disturbed, he would look at her. She would have been less confused if he had looked with spite, or even hatred.

This was different and infinitely more worrying. He must

106

recognise her. He was neither feverish nor delirious. When he spoke, it was in a reasonable manner.

But he looked at her as if she were not his wife, as if she were some indifferent being, some object. Not even that! Because his gaze was clear. He was not looking at external appearances, at the fresh cheeks beginning to become blotchy beneath the powder, the pretty pale-blue eyes, the fleshy lips. He was looking right inside her—she felt it.

Indeed, she was convinced that he had guessed her anxiety and was allowing her to struggle with her own conjectures.

He was not mad and yet he was not himself; he was no longer Malétras.

He felt no more hatred or affection, no scorn or sarcasm.

He saw her naked, as she really was, as she had never even seen herself, and what he saw was a matter of indifference to him.

The proof that she was not mistaken came that evening. At seven o'clock Verel and Devismes were announced. They were, in a way, the official delegation from the Cintra. Steuvels should really have come, since he had closer links with Malétras, but he had chosen not to. He had a weak heart too, and the atmosphere of a sick-room might have affected it.

'You can go up, doctor. You too, Monsieur Devismes. I think my husband will be pleased to see you.'

She went ahead of them, and entered first to announce the visitors and make sure everything was in order. He did not blink, just looked at them as he looked at his wife. Devismes, after a few words suited to the occasion, could not think of anything else to say. Verel's nervous tic was more obvious than ever.

'Well! Lets hope that you'll be in your usual place at the Cintra next week. Eh, Verel?'

'There's no reason why he shouldn't be.'

He listened. He heard. His face remained still. No doubt he could imagine the arguments amongst the bridge players to decide which of them would take on the duty.

It would have been less painful to see him in a bad temper or bitter. But he just seemed to be thinking of something else as the two of them stood by his bed.

'I suppose you've written to my daughter?' he said to Hermine.

He knew she had. It was not a question. He was sure. He did not hold it against her. He accepted events and visits, words and smiles addressed to him, encouragement and promises, all as part of a mechanism apart from and indifferent to him.

'Well, old man, have a good rest. Get back on your feet soon, and come and drink your port with us.'

They fled, in a hurry to be outside, to be back in the comforting world they were used to.

'Come into my sitting room for a moment, doctor. Do you mind, Monsieur Devismes? Tell me, Monsieur Verel, what do you think?'

'About what?'

'Malétras. You know what I mean. You probably know him better than I do.'

Verel hung on to platitudes.

'I wonder if it's not just a reaction. You forget that he has been severely shaken.'

'Do you really think so?'

She knew that he would turn away. He searched for something else to say.

'One mustn't forget that Malétras has always been a very unusual person. He's someone who has never confided in anybody.'

'You can't convince me that something hasn't changed. When he looks at me, I'm frightened sometimes. Listen, doctor. You're his friend. He won't find it odd if you come to see him often. I'd like you to examine him from that point of view. I spoke about it earlier to Professor Picard.'

'What did he say?'

'That it was more your department than his.'

Verel submitted.

'I'll come and see him. But you mustn't get any ideas. I'm convinced that in a few days, when he's up and about . . . Remember that this man has probably never stayed in bed in his life.'

'I know.'

She was not convinced. So little so that when she was eating alone in the dining room, she was still thinking about it.

'Tell me, Rose . . .'

'Yes, madame.'

'The moment you've brought in the dessert, I'd like you to go up to monsieur to ask if he needs anything. Manage it so that you stay in the room for a bit. Has the nurse had supper?'

'Yes, madame. She eats at six o'clock.'

'Your excuse can be to clear up then.'

'She didn't want to eat in the room, and we put up the folding table in madame's bathroom.'

'It doesn't matter. You don't understand. I'm asking you to linger for a while in the room and observe monsieur. Without seeming to, of course! Come and speak to me afterwards.'

'Yes, madame.'

A few minutes later, Rose came down again and stood near the dining-room door.

'Well, Rose? What did monsieur say to you?'

'He didn't say anything, madame.'

'What was he doing?'

'He was looking at himself in the mirror and passing his hand over his face.'

'You didn't go out right away?'

'I stayed at the end of the bed for a good while.'

'Didn't he get impatient?'

'No, madame. He didn't appear to see me.'

'Didn't he look at you?'

'Yes, madame.'

'Didn't you think that . . . well . . . didn't you get the impression that monsieur was . . . was different from his usual self?'

'Oh, yes, madame! I did this morning. I said so to Eugénie. I said you could have dropped the tray down in front of him and he wouldn't have flinched. It's not like . . .'

'Thank you, Rose.'

At nine o'clock the doorbell rang. It was Philippe, Malétras's nephew, who did not know anything had happened and had come to return two of the five hundred francs he had borrowed.

'Is my uncle not here, Aunt?'

'He's in his room. Your uncle has been very ill. He nearly died. He's feeling better now. What did you want with him?'

'It's private, Aunt.'

'I'll ask him if you can come up.'

Malétras was not asleep. Hermine, tactfully, did not remain during the conversation, but she thought that her husband looked at the long-haired young man more deeply and insistently than he had the other visitors.

'Come in, son.'

She was struck by the word, and went out.

'I'm sorry to disturb you, Uncle. I didn't know. I wanted, as I promised . . .'

Malétras frowned, as if trying to remember, and then asked a question.

'Did your friend Jean Gancel stay there?'

'He has come back.'

'Has he seen his girlfriend?'

'Yes. It's been fixed. Monsieur Gancel has allowed them to meet once a week, in his presence, until . . .'

The young man stopped, because it seemed to him that his uncle was not listening. What particularly embarrassed him was to feel a sharp look gliding over his face, scrutinising every detail; its intensity made it so tangible that Philippe passed a hand over his cheeks as if to remove something.

'Go on.'

'I've brought you two hundred francs instead of one, because Jean paid for my return ticket.'

He put the notes on the bedside table.

'I'll come back next month. I do thank you, Uncle. I think it's thanks to you that Jean didn't . . . didn't . . .'

'And your mother?'

'She's well.'

'Your father?'

'My father too.'

'Did you tell them you were coming to see me?'

'No. They don't know.'

'You can tell them I've been very ill.'

'Yes, Uncle. My mother will certainly come.'

'If she likes.'

'Good night, Uncle.'

'Good night, Philippe.'

Malétras had asked Philippe for news of his father and mother, something he had never done before. Why? And why, above all, had he done so in that indifferent tone?

A year earlier Philippe had read a novel in which a character had appeared who was described as 'impassive.' He had liked that word. He had wanted to become impassive. For several days he had observed himself, and tried to keep a neutral expression on his face.

He had been unable to. People are never neutral. Even if one is just greeting somebody on the other side of the street, one automatically gives a slight smile, showing some feeling, whether of pleasure, respect, or surprise.

Malétras had asked him for news of Jean Gancel, of his father and mother, but not for a second could he sense the slightest feeling.

'You saw your uncle? How did you find him?'

'Well, Aunt.'

'Did he say anything special?'

'No, Aunt.'

'Good night, Philippe.'

And Malétras was again alone in his bed, with his mirror at hand on the satin coverlet.

Laniel came to Rue de la Commanderie, while Berthe went to her seamstress. He had to wait because the barber was there. Hermine thought it more discreet to remain in the boudoir, unless someone asked to see her.

'Good morning, Father. Berthe and I heard . . .'

It was as though Malétras had read his wife's letter, listened to the conversation in the glassed-in office in the garage, heard the consultation on the telephone with Professor Picard. He was not surprised, or angry, or impatient, or sardonic.

'Sit down.'

'It's not worth it. Berthe is waiting for me. She was very upset at the news of your illness, and if you're not against it, and if . . . if Hermine has no objection . . . she'd like to come and tell you herself.'

'She can come.'

They could all come, all of them, and his first wife's relations, the poor sisters-in-law, the shabby brothers-in-law, they could even dress up their brats and drill them before bringing them to wish their uncle Malétras the best of health.

None of it mattered. When anyone came in, and when the person went out again, Malétras would turn to the nurse and give a funny, rather conspiratorial look.

It was as if to say:

'Well, we're being disturbed. Here's another one to look at Malétras's carcass in its bed.'

And after they had gone:

'There, we're in peace now.'

And he would take up the thread of his dream that was not really a dream; he would return to his world, his very own world, the only real one.

The rest had no substance. For years and years he had lived with these people, with relations, friends; he had handled a lot of business, signed thousands and thousands of papers, handled millions of francs; he had watched over things, been worried, excited, overjoyed.

Now he was over sixty and he realised that none of it existed. He had certainly felt that two nights before, while the three others waited to see if he would die or not. He had searched stubbornly, desperately, alone with himself, for something to cling to, even a memory, and he had found nothing. In the end the only reality he could find was the fly on his face and a few impressions of his childhood.

'I think it's time for my medicine, Madame Hamon.'

He spoke gently to her. She had rarely had such a polite and gentle patient. And yet she too felt ill at ease alone with him in the room.

'I'll go and fetch Berthe and I'll come back right away.'

'Did she bring the children?'

'She didn't want to tire you. Another day, if you'll allow it.'

He saw his daughter, looked at her carefully, and was surprised that this already plump person should be his child. She was elaborately dressed. She seemed to attach the utmost importance to everything that denoted social station, to make sure her dress came from such and such a shop, that she had the same earrings as Madame So-and-so.

She thought it necessary to wipe her eyes, which were not damp.

'If you knew, Father, what I felt . . .'

And then? She did her little circuit, like the others, and when she went, Malétras turned to the door, as if to say:

'Next!'

There was, in fact, someone else, who had been waiting for a quarter of an hour in Hermine's drawing room. It was Gancel, who did not think it necessary to say anything, but just clasped his friend's hand for a long time and then sat by the head of the bed with his hat on his knees.

He had never looked so thin and feeble. One could literally smell death in him. And yet he did not look defeated, or even resigned. He was fighting. He wanted to be brave to the end.

They looked at one another: they were the same age, they had led more or less parallel lives, been through the same struggles, and ended up at more or less the same point.

Malétras looked around for Madame Hamon, who remained discreetly by the window. It was an automatic glance. Even if she

112

had not been there he would not be able to do what, for a second, he longed to do.

Yet he was tempted. His hand held the ivory handle of the mirror, which belonged in Hermine's dressing case.

He wanted to look at himself once more, compare his decay with Gancel's, to measure on each face the marks left by life.

What could they have said to each other?

'Well, Gancel?'

'Yes, well! What do you think then? What do you think about it all, what we've done, what we've achieved, the point we've reached? Eh? What do you think about it?

'Your wife is ill. Your daughter is ugly and disagreeable. Your son is about to marry a tart. And you, one fine morning, will be taken to the cemetery, in style.

'Well? Don't you sometimes rebel? Don't you sometimes . . .

'Listen, Gancel! Something extraordinary has happened to me—Malétras. Extraordinary for those who don't realise, who live their lives mechanically. Would you believe that I started going every evening to see a girl who wasn't even pretty, an unhealthy and unintelligent little female, and that it became so necessary to my life—to such an extent to my whole life—that I killed her?

'Yes, I, Malétras. It's not as extraordinary as one might think. The proof is that afterwards I went on prowling around her area, and I finally ended up with an old procuress. . . . What did you say? . . . Yes, an old procuress . . . Why? . . . Ha! Ha! Well . . . Why? . . . Well, perhaps you could tell me why? . . . Why have you worked all your life and why do you consider that your daughter, who is ugly and stupid, I can assure you, is worth making sacrifices for?

'I went to the old lady each evening because that had become my life, and one fine evening . . . You didn't understand anything when I rang your doorbell, when you were all three so put out at seeing Malétras. . . .

'No? . . . You don't understand?

'In that case, tell me your secret, because you've certainly got one. In exchange I'll tell you a good trick. . . . Do you remember when we used to swap marbles? . . . Well, we're going to swap tricks, the tricks of life. . . . Yours for mine . . . Mine's easy. . . . You're nice and warm inside the sheets. Your skin is a bit sweaty. Not very, just enough to make you feel sleepy . . .

'You shut your eyes, or you don't. It depends. Both ways work.

You listen to a fly buzzing or you fix on some point seen between your eyelashes.

'Then, particularly if you've been ill when you were little, you . . .'

He did not say any of this. And yet he would have given a lot to know what Gancel's trick was. He must have one. It was impossible that he didn't. Let Gancel look at himself in the mirror, which he must sometimes do, and he would understand that . . .

Malétras was suddenly enraged by his friend's impassivity, and by his own inability to find out his secret. Madame Hamon, who had thought him so good and so gentle, started when she heard him say, in a grating voice:

'So you came to see if I was going to be the one to die first?'

11

It was ten in the morning when he came downstairs for his first outing. It was an event for the whole household, except himself. Rose, who was working in the next room, half opened the door to watch him go by, leaned over the banister, and would no doubt run to the window. Hermine walked down the staircase behind him, looking happy and excited.

'You see, you're as strong as you ever were. You could have gone for a short walk eight days ago.'

It was true, but why did it matter to them, to her, Picard, Verel, and his daughter, who had tried as well? While he had been quite comfortable deep in his bed, they had hatched a sort of conspiracy around him, of which he caught murmurs behind doors.

'Don't you think he's letting himself go, doctor?'

In smooth and gradually more treacherous tones, they asked if he was really feeling so weak, if he would not try to walk a bit, even if it was just to go and sit in the sun in the garden. All those who lived in the house, or even came to it, attacked the final bastion, his room, his bed.

He resisted with all the force of inertia. They tried in vain to call the nurse to witness in front of him.

'Isn't it true, Madame Hamon, that he's as strong as anyone else and that it's staying in bed now that's going to weaken him?'

The nurse did not dare join forces against him. She did not dare support him either, for fear of appearing to defend her job.

Even one of his first wife's sisters, Félicie, Philippe's mother, came to help.

'My goodness, Jules, I wonder if you're not letting yourself go. You don't look like a man who should be in bed.'

She had spoken to him of his sisters, his brothers and brothers-in-law.

'Everybody is worried about you and your illness. They would like to come and see you, but they're afraid of bothering you.'

It was a conspiracy. Hermine must be taking the visitors aside at the bottom of the stairs.

'Try to distract him. His apathy is what's undermining his strength. He's not interested in anything, doesn't want anything. He could have been up for the last week, but he insists on staying in bed.'

Verel came from the Cintra to talk to him: according to him, the little group of bridge players missed him greatly. Nobody knew what to invent, or who to call to the rescue. And all this because it frightened them to see a man peacefully in bed, sufficient unto himself, looking coldly at the people around him, like a goldfish watching men from its bowl.

No doubt if he had insisted on getting up and going out, a conspiracy would have been mounted in the opposite direction; they would have proved to him that he was too weak, that he still needed to be careful, that since it was for the sake of his health he must not mind spending a few extra days in his room.

He could have brushed it all aside with a word, a gesture, but it was not worth it. He listened to them without answering. A lot of people had been to see him, because the *Phare du Havre* had published a paragraph announcing his illness and wishing him a prompt recovery. The Poineaus had come, and others, people from the bank, his successors at the Docks, former employees.

One day when she was in the room at the same time as Hermine, Rose, who was near the window, saw something in the street and immediately called her mistress with a discreet gesture. Hermine looked too, and hesitated. It was a mystery, which had already been talked about between them.

'You should come and have a look at this man.'

He was not in bed at that moment, but sitting on a couch while his bed was being aired.

'Rose has been telling me about him for several days. Apparently he spends his days prowling around the house. When he's not out on the street, he's in the café, but he never stops staring at our windows.'

He had gone to look, more for the sake of peace than out of curiosity, because he knew already that it was Joseph. And indeed it was he. He had a plaster on his neck again. He looked nervous and discouraged.

'You don't know him, do you? You don't know what he wants with us?'

Malétras had shrugged his shoulders. Then he gave in to all of them, not because of Joseph, who was probably in the street watching him, but because these little manoeuvres were beginning to bore him.

All right, he was no longer ill. Just because he had got dressed like everybody else was no reason to surround him with exclamations of amazement.

'Don't you think, Rose, that monsieur looks well?'

'Yes, madame.'

'He's got a little bit thinner. But you notice that only around the waistcoat! A few walks in the sun and . . . Wait for me, I'll get my hat. . . .'

No! Not that! He was quite happy to go for a walk, since he was being sent out for some fresh air like a child or a dog, but he did not want to be taken for a walk.

'I prefer to go out alone.'

'But if . . .'

'I said I will go out alone.'

He said it simply, gently, without raising his voice, but he looked at her with those new eyes, as Hermine called them.

She escorted him down the stairs. He went into the hall, and then turned back and entered his study, while his wife watched him from the doorway. He could have shut the door. He could have done anything. But it was just because people were of no importance to him that he did not bother to oppose them or even to hide. In front of Hermine, to her great astonishment and anxiety, he took out his chequebook and put it in his pocket.

'You won't stay out long, will you? The first outing must be short. You're not ill any more, but staying in bed will have weakened you.'

She was going to follow him; he was sure of that. Or else, if she did not dare, she would send Rose on his heels. He did not turn around to see. He walked as he had done in the past. He made a move towards the cigar case in his pocket, but it was no longer there; Professor Picard had expressly forbidden tobacco, threatening him with a new attack if he smoked.

It seemed that his step had changed. He no longer walked like someone going somewhere, but like a man wandering anywhere, aimlessly, and that was extraordinary, because it had never happened to him, before, even when he had had nothing to do.

He looked at the houses, the open windows, the sheets and bedcovers being shaken out in the sun, a servant in a striped waistcoat polishing the brass knocker on a front door.

Warm air enveloped him like a murmuring caress. He could sense a busier life going on far away, he could guess at the sea down there behind blocks of houses, that vast breathing surface, silent and glittering. He listened with delight to the din of a tram he could not yet see, which foretold the lively streets of the centre of town, which he was approaching, and at that moment he saw Joseph walking slightly ahead of him on the opposite pavement.

Joseph did not hide, but did not push himself forward either. Malétras turned left, and Joseph quickly did the same. Malétras passed him, and Joseph walked faster. At a corner, Malétras stopped, and the other man stopped as well, confused, looking at him anxiously. He was pale. He had rings around his eyes. It was he who appeared to have been ill, and his step betrayed his nervous state.

He was disturbed when Malétras openly crossed the street, came towards him, and said:

'Well?'

He had the look of a guilty man trapped. What was he afraid of? Why did he appear to be looking around him for help?

'I'm sorry. I didn't want to embarrass you by approaching you in the street. I thought . . .'

What did he think? He thought that Malétras would understand his manoeuvre and discreetly lead him to an out-of-the-way place before speaking to him, towards the quays, for example, where a previous interview had taken place.

'Were you afraid I'd die?'

The words were harsh but they were said without irony or malice. It was an observation, and an indifferent one, more than a question. At the same time, Malétras, as he had expected, saw

117

at a little distance the figure of Rose, with a ridiculous red hat perched on her head.

'It's not what you think, Monsieur Malétras. All the same, I must talk to you.'

'Let's walk.'

'In the middle of town?'

They had reached Rue de Paris and could see the heavy façade of the bank where Malétras was a director.

'Tell me.'

Joseph could not, just like that, on the spur of the moment. It was as though he was ashamed of walking in the street beside a man like Malétras, whom several people had already greeted. His appearance was unprepossessing, of course. He did not look like a vagabond or a delinquent. He was dressed quite decently. But something about him was anxious, agitated, unwholesome, and he must have been conscious of it, because he tried to avoid people's stares.

'You must have been very frightened?'

Joseph shot little glances at him that were hard to define. Admiration seemed to mingle with fear and envy. Most of all, there was amazement at Malétras's total serenity.

'I understand why you might think that. It's wrong. I can assure you that you are mistaken about me.'

They were passing a big café, and Malétras, who never sat in sidewalk cafés, decided to sit down there. He went to a table, planted himself in a wicker chair, sighed comfortably, and stretched his legs.

'Sit down.'

Rose was confused and did not know where to go; she hesitated on a corner, trying to hide.

'What will it be, gentlemen?'

'A glass of beer.'

'Me too,' Joseph stammered.

From time to time the breeze would gently swell the striped awning beneath which they sat. The passers-by almost brushed against them. The foam was creamy white in the glasses on brown felt mats.

'How much do you want?'

'I swear to you, Monsieur Malétras . . . Oh! Sorry . . .'

'What for?'

'I said your name by mistake.'

'Well?'

118

'Oh, good . . . I thought . . .'

He was surprised and upset at the same time. He no longer understood. He no longer knew what to say.

'Yes, perhaps for a moment I had the idea . . . It's hard to explain. . . . You see, I know myself. . . . When I've got money in my pocket, I can't control myself. . . .'

Malétras looked at him, and the other tried in vain to escape this transparent stare.

'I can tell you what my idea was. . . . I've always dreamt of having a brasserie. Not a grand one like this . . . But a clean place, cheerful, full of people . . . So one fine day, when the occasion arose, I would have asked you . . .'

'Have you changed your mind?'

Joseph lowered his head and mumbled:

'I can't any more.'

Then he was silent, as if he had just made a major confession.

'What can't you do any more?'

He looked up. He could not believe that Malétras was asking that question so calmly and simply.

'I can't stay in Le Havre any more.'

'Are you afraid?'

'I'm unhappy.'

And suddenly, cracking his fingers, pulling on them in a paroxysm of nerves:

'I miss Lulu.'

They were silent. Malétras once again reached for his cigar case.

'That surprises you, doesn't it?'

Then, letting out his innermost thoughts:

'I don't know how you manage. When I heard that you were ill, I thought . . .'

'What did you think?'

'You know. . . . Or else . . .'

If Malétras did not understand that, it was more staggering than anything!

'Do you want to go away?'

'Yes.'

'Where?'

'I don't know . . . To another country. . . . Here I miss her. It gets worse every day. . . . I wondered if you would ever recover.'

'Didn't you think of ringing my doorbell?'

'How can you suppose . . .'

'Waiter,' called Malétras, 'bring me a pen and some paper.'

A red writing pad with an advertisement on it was brought as well, but he pushed it away. They were right in the middle of town. Malétras could still see the housemaid's red hat here and there in the moving crowd, as she swam against the current.

He did not hide. Joseph could not believe his eyes. He spread out his chequebook on a corner of the table, filled in the blanks, hesitated about what number to write in.

'How much?' he asked.

It looked as if he would obediently write in any number.

'Whatever you judge right.'

The word struck Malétras, and he observed Joseph for a long time before writing again.

'There. I've made it payable to the bearer. The bank is right there. You can cash it later on.'

Joseph did not dare to look. He had vaguely read 200,000 or 300,000. He was in a hurry to leave. He shook from head to foot but did not yet dare leave his chair.

Malétras, who had drunk a large mouthful of beer and was wiping his moustache, was pursuing a new idea.

'Where is she?'

And Joseph said in a low voice, casting guilty looks around him:

'You needn't be afraid.'

'What did you do with her?'

'I couldn't carry her by myself.'

'Of course.'

'And I didn't want to put myself at someone else's mercy either.'

'So?'

'I had to cut her up.'

'Oh.'

Malétras looked at him more carefully than ever, with cold curiosity. It was odd. Joseph may have been afraid of talking about these things, but he appeared less upset than before.

'I miss Lulu,' he had just said quite sincerely.

He could speak her name. He could conjure up the hideous scene. For him, the material details had no importance.

'One part is in one of the docks at the port and one in another. . . . The most dangerous part was the head.'

'Well?'

'When I went to Nice, I stopped in Paris for a few hours. . . .

You understand? . . . Like that, if they find one part . . . I went to the Saint-Martin canal.'

Malétras really wished he had a cigar at that moment. He made a sign with his head that he understood, that it was all over.

'You wanted to know. . . .'

'Thank you.'

'I'll probably catch a boat to America. . . .'

Malétras was watching the procession of passers-by, and the other man did not know how to take his leave.

'I did what I could. . . .'

One question was burning on his lips. He could think of no decent way to ask it. He went on shyly observing the man sitting opposite him.

'You'll stay in Le Havre?'

Malétras understood. He simply nodded. He called the waiter.

'What do I owe you?'

'Four francs, monsieur.'

He paid, looking in his waistcoat pocket for a ten-sou piece for the tip.

'I'll say good-bye. . . .'

Standing up, Malétras nodded again, indicating that it was all right, that his companion could go. It was as if he was no longer thinking about him.

'I promise you'll never hear me mentioned again. . . .'

'Good-bye.'

And Malétras calmly joined the crowd flowing along the pavement. Joseph stood for a long time watching him, hoping that perhaps he would turn round, but he did not turn, and Rose rushed off down a cross-street.

They saw him again at the Cintra at the cocktail hour. On the first day, Emile, the waiter, rushed up to him, smiling, with happy words of welcome on his lips. Malétras looked at him. He looked at him simply, coldly, in the way he looked at everybody, and the waiter went off towards the counter with his head down.

One day, on Rue de Paris, a girl, walking fast, almost bumped into him. She raised her head to apologise and smiled, hesitating before speaking to him, as though she felt she should show some small sign of recognition. It was Martine.

He had seen her too. He had looked at her. Exactly as though she were an object, a chair or a lamppost.

'By the way, Madame Maria, I met the gentleman . . . you know . . . the one who . . .'

'He passed by here yesterday.'

'Did he say hello to you?'

Old Maria's face showed that he had not said hello, and that he had looked at her too.

'I was quite startled.'

He went back once, just once, to the Poineaus'; it was to tell them that, although he was leaving his money in the business, he could no longer take a personal interest in it.

He could be seen walking around, sitting in sidewalk cafés, sometimes for hours, or else on a bench, in the sun, by the sea, in a square, anywhere.

Hermine was afraid of him; he knew that. She saw Verel often. Verel, at the Cintra, observed him as one might observe a sick person.

Malétras knew that too. And even that his wife and daughter were reconciled. The anxiety had brought them together.

'What does Verel say?'

'He won't commit himself. . . .'

'Do you think something really happened?'

'Why would he have given that man three hundred thousand francs?'

'Did you ever see him again?'

'Never. And I found other irregularities in his bank account that I can't explain.'

'My husband admitted to me yesterday that my father once borrowed some money from him.'

They were too kind to him. It was ridiculous. They waited on him hand and foot, as if he were ill. They watched him through the window when he went out. When he remained too long alone in a room, Rose would be sent to see what he was doing.

None of this escaped Malétras, but he was indifferent to it. His world went with him. He could isolate himself without even closing his eyes, on whatever bench he was sitting, whatever café chair. He did not need the flies any more. He could sink at will into a semi-torpor, which would soon be filled with sounds, colours, smells.

'A bouquet, monsieur?'

It was the end of June or the beginning of July. He had heard, the night before, that Gancel was dying.

'Won't you go and see him?' Hermine had asked.

'No.'

'He came when you were ill.'

He had not replied.

He was at his favourite café, in full sun. He was staring fixedly at something, but he saw nothing. There were a lot of people around him, who were talking, but he heard only the flower-seller's cry:

'A bouquet, monsieur?'

He was unable to say at first what scent it was that he was breathing. He could vaguely see white, red, and pink flowers. He did not move. But a moment later, he was trying to follow a difficult path into the unknown; he breathed deeply and found himself lying in a garden in the shining grass, and right next to him, against him, was a bank of carnations, quivering with buzzing insects.

It was eight days before his first communion. Every afternoon he used to go to the priest, who would receive him in the presbytery garden. On the other side of the bank of carnations, opening into the stone wall, was the dark, cold corridor that led to the sacristy; the smell of incense mingled with that of the flowers.

Why had he cried with joy, lying stretched out in the sun?

'Is the chair free, monsieur?'

He did not answer, and they must have thought he was asleep. He heard glasses being placed on the table, but, more clearly, he heard the bees buzzing from one carnation to another, and the harmonium.

'Gancel is dead,' his wife said when he returned that evening. 'I arrived just at the moment when the priest was coming in for the last rites.'

He went to the funeral. The absolution was sung in the church of Saint-Séverin; a stained-glass window created a dazzling fireworks effect.

Malétras went for a walk every day, taking small steps. He was becoming thinner. His waistcoat was loose over his stomach.

Once again it was Eugénie who betrayed him.

'Madame won't believe this! Yesterday, when I was doing the shopping, I saw monsieur. . . .'

'Well, Eugénie?'

'I tell you, madame won't believe it. I saw monsieur going into the church of Saint-Séverin. I was so amazed that I went in a little after him. There was nobody in the church. Except him. All alone on the right-hand aisle, by a confessional.'

The following Sunday he went to church.

In the autumn, he again rose in the morning at five-thirty, as he used to, and went to the first mass every day.

He neither concealed it nor showed off about it.

He remained the same—docile, indifferent.

One evening, Hermine murmured, smiling to encourage him: 'I knew you'd end up believing in God.'

He looked at her. He said:

'No.'

And he turned his back on her and did something else.

Hermine died five years later. Malétras outlived her by seven years, during which he kept only Eugénie to look after him in the big house on Rue de la Commanderie, where most of the rooms were closed up. She went on hating him as much as ever.